Nelly the MONSTeR Sitter

To the Greenhalghes at number twelve

A Catalogue record for this book is available
from the British Library

ISBN 0 340 88434 7

Typeset in Baskerville by Avon DataSet Ltd,
Bidford-on-Avon, Warwickshire

Printed and bound in Great Britain by
Bookmarque Ltd, Croydon, Surrey

The paper and board used in this paperback by
Hodder Children's Books are natural recyclable products made
from wood grown in sustainable forests. The manufacturing
processes conform to the environmental regulations
of the country of origin.

Hodder Children's Books
A division of Hodder Headline Ltd
338 Euston Road
London NW1 3BH

Nelly the MONSTER Sitter

Huffaluks, Muggots & Thermitts

KES GRAY

Illustrated by Stephen Hanson

Hodder
Children's
Books

A division of Hodder Headline Limited

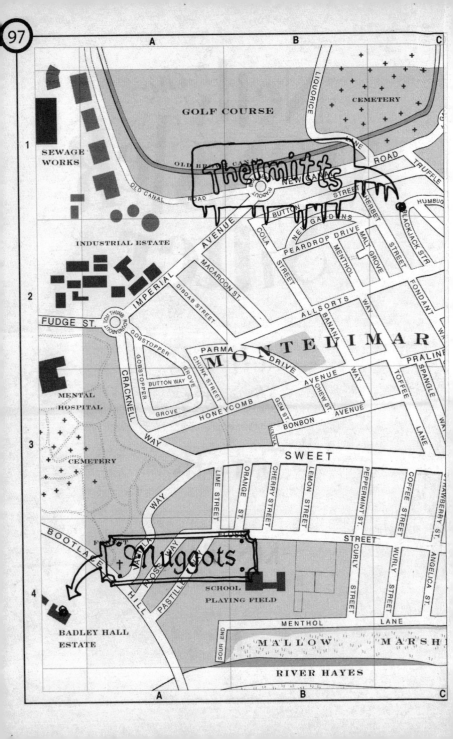

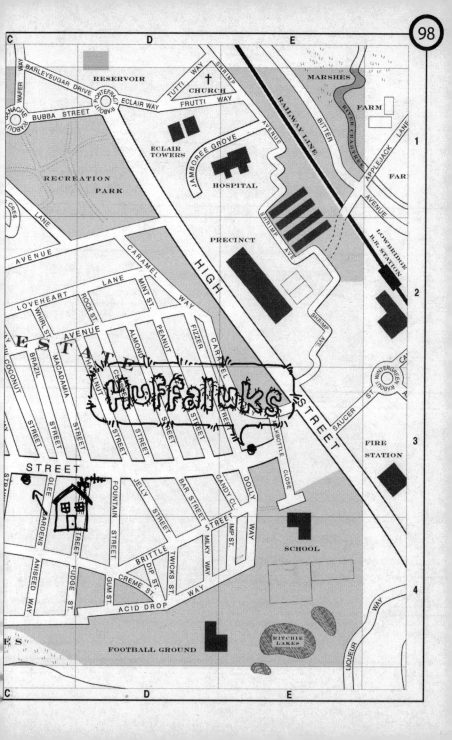

NELLY THE MONSTER SITTER

'If monsters are real, how come I've never seen one?' said Nelly.

'Because they never go out,' said her dad.

'Why don't monsters ever go out?' said Nelly.

'Because they can never get a baby sitter,' said her dad.

Nelly thought about it. Her mum and dad never went out unless they could get a baby sitter. Why should monsters be any different?

'Then I shall become Nelly the Monster Sitter!' smiled Nelly.

1

It was Nelly's twelfth birthday. The sun was shining, the birds were singing, but there was one small problem. It was Asti's twelfth birthday as well.

'I want to go clothes shopping,' said Asti.

'Well I don't,' said Nelly. 'I want to go ice skating.'

'Well I don't,' said Asti. 'Ice skating is stupid. All you do is fall over and get your bum wet and your hands cold.'

'It's not as stupid as clothes shopping,' said Nelly. 'All you do is try things on, take things off, try things on, take things off, and when you do find something you like, get told they haven't got it in your size.'

'At least you can't get your fingers sliced off, clothes shopping,' said Asti.

Nelly the Monster Sitter

'Shame you can't get your head sliced off,' muttered Nelly.

'MUM! DAD! Did you hear what Nelly just said? She said she wanted to cut my head off!' bleated Asti.

Nelly's mum and dad admonished Nelly with a crunch of toast and a weary jiggle of their eyebrows.

'What about paint balling?' said Nelly. 'Craig went paint balling for his birthday and said it was brilliant fun.'

Asti's face crumpled at the very thought. 'There is no way I'm going paint balling on my birthday, or any day for that matter. You get paint all over you, and Natalie says it really stings when the bullets hit you. She ended up with bruises all over her.'

'That's 'cos nobody likes her,' said Nelly.

'I like her,' said Asti.

'Nobody normal likes her,' mumbled Nelly.

'MUM! DAD!' squawked Asti. 'Did you hear what Nelly just said? She said I'm not normal!'

Nelly's mum and dad chastened Nelly with slurps of coffee and weary rolls of their eyes.

'OK, let's go shoe shopping instead!' said Asti, hitting upon an ingenious compromise.

'Shoe shopping is the same as clothes shopping!' protested Nelly.

'No it isn't,' said Asti. 'Because with clothes shopping you're shopping for *clothes* but with shoe shopping you're shopping for *shoes*!'

Nelly stared speechless at her mum and dad, but both had gone into hiding behind their morning newspapers.

'You can't wear clothes on your feet, can you?' said Asti, sensing that she was on to a winner with this one. 'And you can't wear shoes on your body, can you?' she said, forcing the point home.

'Yes, but you still have to traipse from shop to shop shopping for them, don't you?' argued Nelly.

'Different type of shops,' countered Asti.

Nelly stared into her breakfast bowl and wondered whether it was possible to adopt a cornflake as a second sister. At least that way she could enjoy some intelligent conversation once in a while.

'You're the same *every* year,' sighed their mum, lowering her newspaper. 'You can never agree on anything. Whatever one of you wants to do on your birthday, the other one doesn't want to do it. You've always been the same, ever since you were toddlers. If Dad and I suggested going to a safari park, one of you would develop an instant fear of lions. If we suggested going to the cinema, one of you would rather have a picnic in the park.'

'If we suggested a birthday meal, one of you would want to go to a pizza restaurant, and the other would want to go to a burger bar,' confirmed Dad.

'Or one of you would want to eat bamboo shoots and the other one would want to eat octopus toenails,' exaggerated Mum.

'You have never, ever, ever been able to agree on what to do on your birthday,' sighed Dad.

'That's why we always end up having a barbecue at home.'

'I'm sure you just do it to spite one another,' said Mum. 'When you were toddlers we couldn't even get you into a ball pool, because one of you wanted only red balls and the other wanted yellow balls.'

'You're twins, for goodness' sake,' said Nelly's dad, about to touch upon a rather sensitive topic. 'You're supposed to like the same things, wear the same clothes, share the same thoughts!'

'No I am not!' said Nelly, slamming the back of her spoon into her cornflakes. 'I'd rather die than be like Asti.'

'Yes, well I'd rather die than be like you,' said Asti, more than happy to return the compliment.

'Well I'm not going shopping,' said Nelly.

'And I'm not going ice skating,' said Asti, 'or paint balling, or anything that you want to do.'

'And I'm not doing anything that you want to do either,' said Nelly, folding her arms and leaving her cornflakes to go soggy. 'Actually, what about bowling?'

Asti wavered and then held out her hands. 'I might break my nails.'

'Aaaaaaaaaarrrrgggggghhhhh!' growled Nelly.

'A barbecue it is then,' sighed Dad.

2

And so the birthday agenda was set. For the twelfth year in a row, it would be the same as usual, with one small exception. There would be a traditional Morton family barbecue at home with both of the twins allowed to invite *one* guest each.

'Why only *one* each?' said Nelly, who hated having to whittle her friends down to anything less than five.

'Because last year you all got carried away and ended up squirting water over the windows with the hose pipe,' said her dad, stepping into the shed and prodding the barbecue with a stick to see if any spiders were lurking inside.

'What's so wrong with that?' said Nelly. 'It was a baking hot day.'

'The windows were WIDE OPEN, that's what was wrong with that!' said Nelly's mum, marching into the shed and taking the barbecue by both handles. 'We ended up with water all over the kitchen floor. And anyway, you're too old for parties now.'

Nelly's dad stepped forward to assist his wife,

but withdrew his hands sharply when a small earwig dropped from the grill tray and tumbled into the bed of cold ash below.

'I thought it was a spider,' he whispered.

'And I thought you were a man,' said Nelly's mum, dispensing with the wheels of the barbecue and carrying it out on to the patio instead.

Nelly's dad limped backwards towards the wheelbarrow. 'I'll get the barbecue coals,' he coughed.

Nelly's mum dumped the barbecue in its traditional position on the patio and brushed her hands on her jeans. She looked optimistically at the morning sun and then frowned with less assurance at the shed door. Clifford had still to emerge.

'It's all right for Asti,' said Nelly, 'she's only got one friend.'

'Where is Asti?' said Nelly's mum, scanning the garden with one eye but keeping her other eye fixed on the shed door.

'Upstairs, I think,' said Nelly. 'She's probably

ringing Natalie Dupre, her one and only single sad friend in the world.'

Nelly's mum nodded but wasn't really listening at all.

'Have you found them, Cliff?' she shouted. 'I think they're under the bench next to the flower pots.'

'Yes, I've found them,' replied a loud but far from confident voice.

Nelly's mum took a stride towards the shed and then stopped as the wheel of the wheelbarrow squeaked into view. The rest of the wheelbarrow emerged slowly, ferrying a bag of charcoal and a box of firelighters. At the furthermost end of the wheelbarrow Clifford followed, gingerly steering each handle with the very tips of his fingers.

Nelly and her mum stepped back as Dad wheeled the barrow next to the barbecue and dropped it on to the patio with a shudder.

'I think there might be a big 'un in there!' he said, hopping back as Nelly and her mum stepped forward.

Nelly lifted the charcoal bag out of the barrow and gave it a thorough inspection. 'There are no spiders on here, Dad,' she said, running her hands across every crease of the packet. 'Just a few cobwebs, that's all.'

Nelly's dad stood beside Snowball's cage and watched anxiously as Nelly picked up the box of firelighters and gave them the all clear too.

'In Australia, one bite from a spider can kill you,' he said, hoping in some small way to justify his phobia.

'Yes, well this isn't Australia, is it, Clifford?' said Nelly's mum, who was having none of it. 'This is Lowbridge. The only thing that Lowbridge has in common with Australia is that the mayor has the same surname as Rolf Harris.'

'The mayor spells his Harris with two "S"s,' said Nelly.

'My point entirely,' said Nelly's mum.

Nelly's dad wondered whether it was worth defending his corner with true stories of killer spiders imported from foreign countries inside banana crates, but wisely decided to drop the subject.

'What shall we cook?' he said. 'Shall we try barbecuing something a bit different today?'

Nelly looked uneasily at her mum. 'Different' was considered a dangerous word in the Morton family household, *especially* in the context of food.

In the past, 'different' had meant dangerously experimental things. For vegetarian Mum it had meant the introduction of tofu, soya mince and pulses. For meat-loving Dad it had meant the introduction of pigs' liver, kidneys and tripe. For Asti, it had meant the introduction of bio yoghurts, goats' cheese and lentils. And for Nelly, pilchards, pomegranates and prunes.

'What did you have in mind?' asked Nelly's mum.

'Well,' said meat-loving Dad, 'howzabout some spicy *chorizo* sausage or some spicy French *Toulouse?*'

'Asti doesn't like spicy,' said vegetarian Mum, 'and I don't like sausage.'

Dad leaned on Snowball's cage and then lapsed into guilty silence as sizzling visions of char-grilled rabbit burgers wickedly wafted through his mind.

'What about some stuffed marrow wrapped in tin foil or some satayed tofu in a dry roasted peanut sauce?' said vegetarian Mum.

Nelly's dad turned pale and developed a nut allergy fast.

'How about barbecuing that spider?' said Nelly, pointing to the wheelbarrow.

Nelly's dad leaped away from the barrow, his arms flailing wildly like a Squurm.

'Only kidding,' said Nelly, underestimating the impact of her joke, but pleased that her distraction tactic had worked.

'Can we just have a normal barbecue?' she asked.

Nelly's dad shook himself down and her mum drifted back into the house with a shake of her head.

'A normal barbecue it is then,' coughed her dad.

3

As Mum set about plundering the freezer drawers for barbecue victims, Nelly found herself despatched to the lounge to pick up the birthday wrapping paper that was still strewn across the floor.

'I'm not picking any of Asti's up!' she shouted, bending down to check a label, before extracting a DVD from its silver and green stripy wrapper. Separating her wrapping paper from her sister's wasn't easy because traditionally, and depressingly, both girls' birthday presents were wrapped in identical fashion. Apparently, by treating both girls equally, relatives and friends alike could avoid any sense of favouritism. Or imagination, for that matter.

This year, Nelly's clever tactic for avoiding

identical presents had been to ask for money. But in a hugely infuriating way, Asti had made the same request and asked for money too. That meant that instead of identical presents, the twins got identical sums of money instead. How annoying was that?

Nelly pulled twenty identical pounds from an identical all-singing all-dancing musical card and then began scrunching two sheets of identical spotty wrapping paper into a ball. As usual, her birthday fortunes had been mixed. Clubbed together with the money she had been saving prior to her birthday, she would now have enough funds to buy herself a new mobile phone. Which was good.

But the next time her gran visited the house she would be obliged to wear her new lilac winter-wear birthday sweater. It was thick, it was Arran wool and it hung like a baboon's knuckles beneath her armpits. Which was bad.

Nelly screwed up the Christmas wrapping paper that her gran had recycled for the occasion and aimed it at the bin in the far corner of the room. As the snowball of paper bounced off the lip of the wastepaper bin, Asti entered the lounge.

'I'm not picking yours up,' said Asti, dropping to her knees to examine a label.

'I'm not picking yours up either,' said Nelly, walking over to the far corner of the room with her birthday cards.

'This piece of Sellotape is yours,' said Asti, rolling it between her fingers and pinging it like a bogey towards the telly.

Nelly curled her toes inside her shoes and then began to arrange her cards along the windowsill.

'Oh look!' she said, squeezing the last one into place against the curtains. 'Fifteen cards for me. What a lot of cards *I've* got this year.'

Asti scanned the floor and did a quick mental count of the cards that were remaining. She'd have been hard pushed to muster ten.

'Your phone was ringing earlier,' Asti said, deviously changing the subject.

Nelly spun round. 'Which phone?' she asked.

Asti smiled inwardly and kept her eyes glued matter of factly to the carpet.

'The freak phone in your bedroom, of course,' she said.

Nelly placed her hands on her hips. 'My monster-sitting phone? When? Who was it? Why didn't you answer it? Why didn't you tell me?' she blustered.

'You were outside with Mum and Dad,' smiled Asti. 'That's why you didn't hear it. Ages and ages it rang for. In fact, it rang for so long, it might even have been an *emergency*!'

Nelly's veins fizzed with fury. 'Well why didn't you answer it to see?' she protested.

Asti rolled two pieces of green wrapping paper into makeshift eyeballs and pressed them into her eye sockets. 'I'm not touching your filthy phone – there's no telling what monster germs and diseases are lurking down that phone line.'

She released the green paper eyeballs and leered like a plague victim as they bounced on to the floor.

'The monsters are more likely to catch something off *you*!' retorted Nelly, striding across the lounge and leaving Asti to pick up the rest of the birthday litter.

'Soooooo sorry,' said Asti with mock sincerity. 'Now you'll never know what ten-headed weirdo was trying to ring you.'

'I can ring "call back," dummy,' said Nelly.

Asti crushed the green paper eyeballs into the palm of her hand and cursed under her breath. She had forgotten all about 'call back'.

'I'm not picking that red envelope up,' she said, 'or that white ribbon.'

But Nelly was out of there.

Nelly had call back to ring.

4

She marched into her bedroom and threw a cautionary glance around her room, just to make sure that Asti hadn't been snooping around. If Asti *had* been in the room, she most certainly *hadn't* made Nelly's bed or picked up the empty milk bottle that Nelly had dumped on her bedside table the night before.

Nelly's fluffy red monster-sitting diary lay unopened on her homework table and her secret drawer was tightly closed. Nelly picked up her monster-sitting phone and sniffed it for signs of cherry lip-gloss. She could rest easy. Her room was Asti free.

With a quick tap tap tap of the recall buttons she perched on her homework table and waited for the identity of the missed monster caller to be revealed.

She recognised the number immediately. It belonged to her good friends Grit and Blob, the Huffaluks living just up the road at number 42. Nelly had monster sat their daughter Freeb on a number of occasions and had forged quite a bond with the hairy little toddler.

With a push of another button, she reconnected the call.

Three rings and a click and a clunk later, a deep growly voice answered the phone.

'Yuuuuuss?' growled the voice. 'Grit and Blob's residence, how may I help you?'

24

'This is Nelly the Monster Sitter's residence,' smiled Nelly, 'how may I help you?'

'NELLYYYY!' boomed Grit, forcing Nelly to hold the telephone receiver away from her ear. 'How nice to hear from you. I phoned you earlier but I couldn't get a reply. I thought you'd gone away.'

'I was downstairs, opening my presents, Grit. It's my birthday today,' said Nelly, inching the receiver closer to her ear again.

'And Asti's!' said Grit.

'Yes – and Asti's,' sighed Nelly.

'Many happy returns to you both from all of us,' growled Grit. 'We hope you have a wonderful day.'

'Thank you, Grit,' said Nelly.

'Goodbye, Nelly,' said Grit, replacing the receiver at his end of the line.

Nelly replaced the receiver at her end too, took one step towards the bedroom door and then stopped and scratched her head. With a chuckle she returned to her phone and dialled again.

'Yuuuuuss?' growled Grit.

'Grit,' interrupted Nelly, 'the reason I was calling *you* was to see why you were calling *me*!'

There was a pause, followed by a growl and a roar of laughter. 'Oh yes! I see, of course, Nelly, please don't worry, I wouldn't want to impose on you on your birthday, good gracious no, Blob and I can make alternative arrangements I'm sure.'

Nelly frowned and deciphered his words as best she could.

'Grit, did you want me to monster sit for you today?' she asked.

Now Grit was good at being growly and good at being hairy, but fibbing had never been his forte.

'Oh no no no,' he blustered, 'I was just ringing you to . . . er . . . wish you happy birthday.'

'Grit, you didn't know it was my birthday,' smiled Nelly.

There was a pause as Grit passed the telephone like a hot potato between all three of his leather-palmed paws.

'Er,' he growled, trying to rethink his fib stategy.

'Er yes, I mean no, I mean, I was just ringing you to see if it *was* your birthday!'

Nelly wasn't fooled at all. 'Grit,' she smiled. 'What time did you want me to monster sit for you? I'll be happy to come over if I can.'

Grit's growls began to waver. 'But Nelly, you can't monster sit for us on your birthday – you must already have made plans.'

'Not entirely,' said Nelly, unconvinced that a twelfth birthday barbecue in twelve years constituted plans.

With his fib strategy completely unpicked, Grit decided to spill the beans.

'Well, Nelly, the thing is, my great-great-grandfather is moving into a new bungalow in Toffee Lane today,' explained Grit. 'Blob and I were hoping to go and help him carry in his furniture, just for a couple of hours this afternoon. He says he can carry it all in himself, but he's a hundred and seventy-three and he's almost blind in one eye.'

Nelly frowned. Being nearly blind in one eye

was serious for a Huffaluk. One eye was all that they had!

'Then you *must* go and help him,' said Nelly, trying to think around her barbecue double booking.

She pulled the phone cord towards her bedroom window and peered down at the top of her dad's head. The rest of him was brushing last year's charcoal ash into a bin bag.

'I know!' she said. 'Why don't you bring Freeb over to us? Freeb can be my special birthday barbecue guest!'

For a moment Grit was totally overcome. 'But she's only three, Nelly. You don't want to hang around with a little Huffaluk on your birthday,' he growled.

But Nelly would hear nothing of it. 'I insist,' she smiled. 'I'm allowed one birthday friend and I would like nothing more than for it to be Freeb. The barbecue usually begins about two, why don't you bring her around just after?'

Grit clapped his two free paws together

gratefully and handed the phone to Blob. After six '*Are you sure, Nelly?*'s and umpteen growls of gratitude, the afternoon's arrangements were finally made.

Excellent! thought Nelly, bouncing down the stairs, through the kitchen and on to the patio. A birthday with a difference at last!

5

Outside on the patio, Nelly found her mum arranging six garden chairs around a wrought-iron table. Her dad was scrubbing the grill tray of the barbecue with a rusty wire brush and Asti was, well, being Asti.

'I heard that,' said Nelly, picking up on the end of Asti's last sentence. 'Craig is not my boyfriend, he's just a friend.'

Asti's lips curled into a deliciously wicked smile. She had already nominated Natalie Dupre as her own barbecue guest and was now laying odds on Nelly's chosen favourite.

'If Craig is just a friend, why have you got his name written on your homework book?' teased Asti.

'Because you wrote it on there,' sighed Nelly.

Asti's eyes flashed mischievously to her mum and then across to the grill tray. 'No I didn't!' she fibbed.

'Yes you did,' said Nelly. 'If I'd written Craig's name on my homework book, I would have spelled it properly, not CRIAG, like you did.'

Asti looked flummoxed for a moment. 'Yes, well I was in a hurry,' she finally conceded.

Mum's eyebrows lifted wearily again and Dad flipped the grill tray over into a bowl of soapy water with a sigh.

'Well, for your information,' said Nelly, 'I shan't be inviting Craig or David Beckham or Johnny Depp or Brad Pitt to the barbecue this afternoon. I have invited Freeb.'

Nelly's mum's eyebrows soared like paragliders, Dad's wrist locked in mid scrub and Asti's jaw fell on to the patio and broke into a million pieces like a piece of fine china.

'You've invited WHO?' she gasped.

'I've invited Freeb,' smiled Nelly. 'She only lives

down the road, and Grit and Blob are going to drop her round just after two.'

'What a lovely idea,' said Mum, wondering whether a wrought-iron seat would be strong enough to support a monster's bottom. 'Do you know what she eats?'

'Us, probably,' squealed Asti, suddenly breaking out into a fit of uncontrollable shudders. 'You can't invite it round here!' she gasped.

'Why not?' asked Dad, refinding his scrubbing action. 'If their home is good enough for our daughter to visit, why isn't our home good enough for their daughter to visit?'

'*Because it's a disgusting, slimy, blood-sucking monster, that's why!*' groaned Asti.

'Hairy, actually,' smiled Nelly.

'Asti, you really must stop making judgements about people before you've even had a chance to meet them,' said Mum. 'It really is a most unsatisfactory approach to life.'

'I'm sure Freeb is a delightful person,' said Nelly's dad, wondering how many mouths the burgers would stretch to. 'Will we need to get some more grub out of the freezer, Nelly?' he asked diplomatically.

Nelly shook her head and smiled. 'Freeb's only three and she's only got one mouth. And anyway, Blob said she was going to bring some jov cheeks and some mungus steaks.'

'How very kind,' said Dad, wondering whether his traditional, home-made barbecue marinade would be up to the job.

'I'm going to be sick,' gurned Asti, clasping both hands to her mouth and running into the house.

She wasn't sick. She was straight on the phone to Natalie.

'It's actually going to be there in the garden with us!' she squawked. 'Sharing our barbecue, touching our things, gunging all over the place on MY birthday! Can you believe it? She's actually invited a twelve-headed freak into MY house on MY birthday!'

Natalie gasped and a frisson of excitement

tingled through her dental brace.

'If you don't want to come to the barbecue any more, I completely understand,' groaned Asti. 'Maybe we should say our goodbyes now, because if I get eaten, this will be the last conversation we'll ever have.'

'I'M COMING, I'M COMING!' said Natalie, who certainly wasn't going to miss out on an opportunity to ogle a monster. 'I'll see you at two!'

Asti put the phone down and stomped furiously up to her bedroom. As she slammed the door, the sparkling barbecue grill tray emerged from the bowl of soapy water for the last time and was propped up on the table to dry in the sunshine. As Dad peeled the rubber gloves from his fingers, Mum set to with a carving knife and some French bread and Nelly began poking freshly sliced crudités through the wire of Snowball's cage. Preparations for the barbecue were well under way.

'I'm going to Freshco's to buy some fizzy

drinks,' said Dad, slapping his rubber gloves over the washing line. 'Is there anything else we need?'

'Jov cheek dressing and mungus sauce!' laughed Nelly.

'Ooh-er,' said Dad, 'I don't think Freshco's have got a monster-food counter!'

6

When the doorbell rang at two o'clock, Nelly was first to the door. She threw it open with a sweep of her arm, only to find Natalie Dupre darkening the doorstep.

'Is it here yet?' said Natalie, barging past Nelly and swivelling her head in all directions.

Nelly sighed. 'It's not an *it*, she's a Huffaluk and her name is Freeb. And no, she isn't here yet.'

'How many heads has it got?' whispered Natalie, flicking her long, blond ponytail over her shoulder and then peering, wide-eyed, into the lounge.

'One,' said Nelly, leaving Natalie in mid snoop to return to the patio.

Natalie caught her up on the back step and

waved politely to Nelly's parents. 'Where's Asti?' she said.

'Behind me,' sighed Nelly's mum, sprouting two more arms as she stepped towards the barbecue to fan the coals. Asti was hiding behind her, doing a passable impression of a shadow.

'Thank God it's only you!' said Asti, stepping out from behind her mum and seizing the presents that Natalie was holding.

'I've got you the same each!' said Natalie. 'So whoever opens theirs first gets the surprise.'

Asti hurled one of the presents at Nelly and then tore greedily at the wrapping of her own pressie. 'It's-a-CD!' she blurted, making damn sure that Nelly would know the contents before she had so much as peeled back a piece of Sellotape.

'You can take them back if you don't like them,' said Natalie. 'I've stuck the receipt to the back of one of them.'

Nelly removed the wrapping paper from her CD and smiled approvingly at the cover.

'I'll keep the CD but I'll probably take my sister back,' she said, moving on to the card.

Natalie snorted with laughter, and then looked shame-faced at Asti.

'Can I get you a drink, Natalie?' said Dad, moving in with an empty glass and a bottle of lemonade.

Natalie nodded enthusiastically and held out her hand. She waited for the bubbles to rise and the lemonade to foam, and then sidled over towards Asti.

'*It*'s not here yet, then,' she whispered.

'Don't even mention *it*,' shuddered Asti. 'I'm going to die when I see it.'

Natalie raised her glass to her lips and gazed vacantly around the garden. The lawn was clipped to bowling-green height, the conifers were lollipop fat and the barbecue was gleaming cherry-red in the sunshine. A medley of 80s chart toppers (Dad's choice) was drifting softly through the open patio doors from the lounge and wisps of charcoal smoke were beginning to wreathe the air.

'We'll wait for Freeb before I put the food on,' said Mum.

'I think we should eat before we get eaten,' muttered Asti.

'That'll be her now!' said Nelly, springing from her chair at the second ring of the doorbell.

Asti's face turned as pale as a Milky Bar as she inched backwards towards the far corner of the patio.

'If they grab you first I'll go for help; and if they get me first, you go for help, OK?'

'OK,' whispered Natalie, brushing a flying ant

from the shoulder of her purple blouse and then fixing her eyes firmly on the kitchen door.

'Meet my good friends, the Huffaluks!' proclaimed Nelly, stepping proudly through the door and ushering her monster guests through with a sweep of her arm.

Nelly's mum and dad stepped across the patio with broad, welcoming smiles and then faltered slightly as the kitchen doorway filled with red fur.

'Goodness!' said Nelly's mum under her breath as the first pair of hairy Huffaluk shoulders squeezed through the door frame.

'This is Grit!' beamed Nelly.

Asti's body stiffened with repulsion as the Huffaluk's single eyeball swivelled towards her like a tomato on a stalk.

'A very happy birthday to you,' growled Grit. 'And a big hello to you, Natalie, too!'

Natalie froze like an ice pop as Grit's dangling red eye swooped barely a centimetre from her nose.

'Pleased to meet you,' she squeaked, as the eye

circled her head twice and then swooped towards the barbecue.

'I've brought some mungus steaks and jov cheeks!' growled Grit, raising a silver-foiled parcel the size of a kerbstone above his head.

'How very kind!' said Nelly's dad, stunned by the size of the parcel and estimating that he was now about three litres short of marinade.

Nelly smiled excitedly as the other members of the Huffaluk family joined them on the patio.

'This is Blob,' smiled Nelly, as the second hairy chest squeezed into view.

'Hello everyone!' Blob growled, lumbering across the patio to present Nelly's mum with a monstrously weird bunch of flowers. 'It's so kind of you to invite us.'

'And this is Freeb!' said Nelly, bending down to greet a mini Huffaluk as she toddled through the door.

'I'm strong!' growled Freeb proudly, lifting two birthday presents above her head.

'I know – I can smell you from here,' mumbled Asti under her breath.

Nelly glared fiercely at her sister and then opened her arms wide. 'Give us a cuddle, Freeby!' she beamed.

'Give Nelly and Asti their birthday presents, Freeb,' growled Blob. 'We do hope you like them.'

Nelly placed her arms around Freeb and then dropped down on to her knees to receive her present.

'For you,' said Freeb, handing Nelly a spherical present wrapped in green spiky paper.

'For you,' said Freeb, turning towards the other end of the patio and mistakenly holding the second present out for Natalie. Natalie giggled at the error and then peered inquisitively at the glistening blue box, tied with a ribbon of silver cord.

'It really is very kind of you to bring us presents, isn't it, Asti?' said Nelly, trying to coax her sister across the patio.

Asti forced the weakest of smiles and stayed rooted to the spot.

'And it's very kind of you to look after Freeb for us, Nelly. We wouldn't dream of not giving you and Asti a present on your birthday.'

Natalie stepped forward and received the present on Asti's behalf. It felt sticky to the touch – like the inside of a lolly wrapper – and as she shook it, it jangled like the contents of a plumber's bag.

'Here you are, Asti,' said Natalie, holding out

the present for her to take. 'I wonder what it is?'

Asti couldn't care less and kept her hands firmly by her sides.

'*Here* you are, Asti!' said Nelly's dad, giving her a sharp nudge in the ribs with his elbow.

With a face like thunder, Asti accepted the present from Natalie.

'What is it?' she shuddered sullenly, as her fingers stuck to the sticky wrapping.

'Open it and see!' said Nelly, looking down at her own present and gingerly prising off the spiky wrapping with her fingers. It was a bit like trying to unpeel a hedgehog.

'Yes, open it and see!' said Natalie, eaten up with curiosity.

'Earrings!' laughed Nelly, getting her own back for the 'it's-a-CD' moment earlier.

All eyes swung towards Nelly as she lifted two tangles of wire, beads and painted pebbles from her circular box. In truth they looked more like wind chimes and were better suited to elephant-sized ears. But Nelly held them up gratefully for all the world to see and admire.

'I made them myself,' growled Blob proudly, pinging her own earrings with her red, hairy paw.

All eyes reverted to Asti, as she slipped the silver cord from her present and discarded it like a banana skin on to the floor.

'Come on, slowcoach!' said Nelly's mum, trying to make light of the moment.

Asti screwed her face up and picked at the present with all the enthusiasm of a princess peeling a frog.

How ungrateful can you get? thought Nelly. I knew she'd be like this.

Pick by pick, grimace by grimace, Asti slowly unprised her present from its wrapping.

'Junk,' she sighed, slowly lifting the earrings halfway out of the box and then dropping them back in with a clatter.

'Cheers a lot,' she muttered, discarding the present with a shrug.

There was a pause. An awful pause. An

awful, embarrassed pause, as everyone at the barbecue found themselves momentarily numbed and stunned by Asti's rudeness.

'I'll need to wash my hands now,' mumbled Asti, avoiding eye contact with anyone as she walked back indoors.

'Me too,' said Natalie, catching her up at the step.

Nelly's dad stared open-mouthed at his daughter's ingratitude and then sprung back into barbecue mode.

'DRINKS!' he said. 'Can I get anyone any drinks?'

Blob and Grit's eyeballs yo-yoed their approval. 'We really should be going soon – we've got lots of furniture to carry this afternoon – but a drink would be very much appreciated, thank you.'

'I'm strong,' said Freeb, picking up a packet of rabbit food with one paw and doing her own impression of a removal man.

'We know you are, darling,' growled Blob,

running two paws lovingly through her daughter's hair.

'I'll tell you what,' continued Blob. 'Why don't I tell you what to do with the flowers, Yvonne, while Grit explains how to cook mungus and jov cheeks to Clifford?'

In a quick switch of responsibilities, Nelly's mum removed her apron and tossed it to Clifford. Clifford hooked the apron strings over his head and despatched Nelly to the drinks counter with a wink.

'Come on, Freeby,' said Nelly. 'Come and try a glass of lemonade.'

'I'm strong,' said Freeb, picking up a bottle of cooking oil and holding it up above her head.

'If you're *that* strong, come and see if you can carry some glasses, then!' smiled Nelly, taking Freeb by the paw.

As the fruit punch poured, the lemonade fizzed, the flower vase filled and the apron strings knotted, Asti and Natalie emerged from the kitchen and regrouped at the far end of the lawn.

'Aren't they hideous?' Asti whispered, throwing a contemptuous glance at Grit's red, shaggy shoulders and three-toed mammoth feet.

'Gross,' whispered Natalie. 'Their eyeballs are horrible!' she whispered. 'And have you seen how many fingers they've got?'

Asti turned her head slowly to covertly glean the answer.

'Four,' whispered Natalie, before Asti could even start counting. 'And that includes two thumbs!'

Asti's face wrinkled like a wet flannel. 'If anyone expects me to go anywhere near that disgusting little fur ball, then they've got another think coming,' she whispered.

'Me too,' squeaked Natalie, scowling across the garden at Freeb.

'What do you think, Freeby?' said Nelly, watching with amusement as the cute little Huffaluk raised her first ever glass of lemonade to her lips. Freeb's eyeball watered like a tinned tomato and her nostrils flared as the first sip of lemonade slipped home.

'It tastes funny,' she growled, raising the glass to her lips again.

Nelly laughed and set about filling the remaining glasses. 'Look, you're stronger than me, Freeby,' laughed Nelly. 'I can only carry two glasses and you can carry three!'

'I'm very strong,' growled Freeb, turning her three-pawed advantage in the direction of Natalie and Asti.

Natalie and Asti shuddered as Freeb toddled across the lawn towards them. 'It's like a gonk gone wrong,' whispered Asti.

'For you, Natalie,' said Freeb, politely offering up three drinks for Natalie to choose from.

'Thank you,' said Natalie, choosing a glass from the middle.

'For you,' said Freeb, turning to Asti.

'Not if your scummy mitts have touched it, it isn't,' hissed Asti, turning her back.

Natalie took a mouthful of lemonade and then peered suspiciously at her glass. With a roll of her eyes and a pout of her lips, she spat it back into her glass.

'There could be all kinds of invisible freak germs crawling all over that glass,' whispered Asti.

Freeb blinked unsurely at the back of Asti's T-shirt and then toddled back to Nelly.

Nelly was hovering beside the barbecue, waiting for her dad to finish taking Grit through the contents of their knife block.

'You need bigger teeth on the blade to cut mungus,' growled Grit. 'Haven't you got any bigger knives than these?'

Nelly's dad peered down at the open food parcel that Grit had placed on the table. The silver-foil wrapping had been peeled open to reveal the mungus – a raw carcass of orange meat scaffolded with long, purple bones.

'There's a saw in the shed,' joked Nelly.

'Excellent idea,' growled Grit, taking it upon himself to retrieve it.

'Are you sure it's meat?' whispered Nelly, handing her dad a glass of fruit punch.

'It's got bones in,' whispered her dad, prodding the carcass with a skewer and then flapping a wasp from the rim of his glass. 'I suppose it must be.'

'Whatever it is, wasps seem to like it,' she said, waving two more of the pesky insects away from the tin foil.

'It's the jov cheeks the wasps are after,' growled Grit, returning from the shed with a ripsaw in his paw. 'Jov cheeks are very sweet you see, Nelly,' he growled. 'We have the same trouble with wasps when we barbecue jov at home. Don't you worry about it though, Blob's flowers will see to them.'

Nelly turned towards the house to see her mum walking nervously out of the kitchen, carrying the vase of flowers at arm's length.

'Your fruit punch, Grit,' said Nelly, not sure which way to turn next.

'These are jov cheeks,' growled Grit, downing the punch in one and lifting the flitch of mungus with his paw to reveal a glistening, syrupy bed of slithery, brown slop.

'It looks like liver!' said her dad, leaning

51

forward to give it a sniff. 'But it smells like coconut!'

Grit pierced a slither of jov cheek with a skewer and then dangled it over the hot coals of the barbecue. It turned fluorescent pink immediately and then bubbled, whistled and split like a roasted chestnut.

'Who wants to try jov cheek?' growled Grit, holding the skewer forward like a fencing épée.

'THEY DO!' cried Nelly, flapping her hands wildly as a small squadron of wasps converged on the end of the skewer.

'I told you so!' growled Grit. 'Make way for the flowers!'

Nelly and her dad stepped back in astonishment as Blob ushered Nelly's mum towards the barbecue with the vase of flowers. The yellow stalks were writhing like a hydra and the jet-black petals were croaking like bull frogs. Nelly's mum stood stiff-armed beside the barbecue and her eyes seemed on stalks of their own as she set the vase down on the table.

Nelly peered inquisitively at the end of the skewer as Grit drew it casually towards the vase. Nelly's mum held her breath; her dad chewed his lip; even Asti and Natalie couldn't help gawping, having moved one step closer to the barbecue.

For as Grit held the skewer to the vase, the

funereal black petals of each flower opened like a fly trap and despatched a flurry of tendrils, whipcracking in all directions. In a flash, the wasps buzzing around the jov cheek were snapped up from the air and devoured by a crunch of voracious petals.

'That's the end of them,' said Nelly's dad, staring wide-eyed at the now waspless end of the skewer.

'Almost,' said Blob, pointing at the stems of the flowers. Everyone moved a step closer still, as one by one the yellow stalks of the flowers digested the wasps whole, sending them like a python's prey down their length before passing them out into the water at the bottom of the vase.

'They've gone white!' gasped Nelly, staring in disbelief at the colourless husks of the dead wasps, floating to the surface of the water.

'That's where geronimoniums get their yellow and black colours,' smiled Grit. 'They suck them out of wasps. Now who wants to try some jov cheek?'

Nelly's mum passed on vegetarian grounds, Natalie and Asti hid behind the conifers, but Nelly and her dad joined Blob and Freeb with enthusiastic nibbles.

'They're delicious,' munched Nelly's dad, licking his fingers, 'but I won't cook the rest till after the burgers, or we'll be full before we start!'

'I'm sure Freeb will try some of your more exotic food, Clifford, but if she doesn't like it, she'll be happy with mungus and jov,' growled Blob.

'Mungus mungus!' growled Grit. 'I'll just carve the mungus and we must be off.'

Blob drank her fruit punch and chatted politely with Nelly's mum while Grit set to with the ripsaw.

'Cook 'em as they are, Clifford,' growled Grit. 'A couple of minutes on each side of each steak. The bones will turn yellow when they're cooked through.'

Nelly's dad's carnivorous instincts surged up the strings of his apron as humungous mungus steak after humungous mungus steak began to pile up on a tray beside the salad bowl.

'If you don't mind me asking, Grit?' drooled Nelly's dad. 'What is a mungus?'

'It's a bit like a leru without the tentacles,' explained Grit.

Nelly's dad stared blankly at the silver foil. Maybe he shouldn't have asked.

With the presents unwrapped, the mungus carved and the vase of geronimoniums in place, Blob and Grit said their fond farewells.

'Goodbye, Nelly, goodbye, Asti, goodbye, Natalie – thank you so much for playing with Freeb this afternoon!' growled Blob.

Asti and Natalie emerged, leaden-footed, from the foliage and waved sullenly back.

'Oh, I'll be playing games with Freeb all right,' whispered Asti out of the corner of her mouth. 'Just you wait and see.'

7

Nelly and Freeb walked hand in paw to the front door and waved goodbye to Blob and Grit.

'We'll be back around four-thirty!' growled Grit. 'Save us some mungus!'

'Jov for me!' laughed Blob. 'I've got a sweet fang!'

Nelly squeezed Freeb's paw and closed the door.

'Would you like me to show you my bedroom, Freeb?' said Nelly. 'I can show you my bedroom and then we can come downstairs again when my dad has finished cooking the barbecue.'

Freeb nodded and then broke away from Nelly to pick up a pair of Wellington boots that had been tucked away in the corner of the hallway.

'I'm strong, Nelly!' she growled, lifting both boots above her head with one paw.

'I know you are, Freeby!' laughed Nelly. 'Come on, let's go upstairs.'

'This is my bedroom,' said Nelly, stepping to one side to allow Freeb to enter her room first. 'Do you like the colour of my room? The Grerks at number fifty-five gave me the paint for it.'

'It's spotty!' growled Freeb, waving her eye-stalk in the direction of each wall in turn.

'That's right!' said Nelly. 'What do you like best, Freeb, spots or stripes?'

'Triangles,' growled Freeb.

'Fair enough,' laughed Nelly. 'Now then, this is where I sleep. See – it isn't hard like your bed, it's soft and bouncy.'

Freeb watched with interest as Nelly placed her bottom on her mattress and bounced up and down a few times.

'And these are my curtains and this is where I do my homework and this is my monster-sitting diary and this is my special monster-sitting phone!' smiled Nelly, picking up the receiver and holding it to her ear.

Freeb's tomato-red eye drifted across Nelly's desk and then spiralled away in the direction of her drawers.

'Have you got any jigsaws, Nelly? I like jigsaws.'

Nelly shook her head and smiled. 'I'm a bit too old for jigsaws, Freeb. I've still got my teddy though, look.'

Nelly flopped over on to her side, slipped her hand beneath her duvet and pulled out a small, white, knitted bear, with hazel brown eyes and a frayed, black, darned nose.

'His name's Marvin.'

Freeb trotted across the carpet and held out her paws. 'Is Marvin strong?' she growled.

'Not really!' laughed Nelly, cradling her teddy into Freeb's arms.

'I'm strong,' growled Freeb.

'ARE YOU ITCHING?' interrupted an unwelcome voice from the bedroom door.

'*YES!* I'M ITCHING!' came a fog-horned reply.

Nelly looked up from her bed. Asti and Natalie

were standing in the doorway, scratching
furiously.

'I'M REALLY ITCHING!' shouted Asti. 'I'M
ITCHING ALL OVER!'

'ME TOO!' cackled Natalie. 'YOU DON'T
THINK WE'VE CAUGHT FLEAS, DO YOU?'

Asti placed her hands on her hips and looked
accusingly at Freeb. 'FLEAS? FLEAS! NOW WHO
COULD WE POSSIBLY HAVE CAUGHT FLEAS
FROM?'

Natalie turned towards Freeb and placed her
hands on her hips too.

'COULD IT BE NELLY'S TEDDY BEAR?'
shouted Natalie.

'NOOOOOOOOOOOOOOOOOO,' droned
Asti. 'MARVIN HASN'T GOT FLEAS.'

'THEN WHERE CAN THE FLEAS BE
COMING FROM?' chortled Natalie.

Asti scratched her arms, then her chest, then
her chin and then her head.

'They must be coming from . . . YOU!' she
shouted, pointing an accusing finger across the

room at Freeb. 'YOU'RE THE SCUMMY FLEABAG THAT'S GOT FLEAS, AREN'T YOU?'

Freeb clutched Marvin to her chest as Asti and Natalie doubled up with a fit of hysterics. Nelly sprang from her bed and slammed the door in their faces.

'Get lost!' she snapped.

'Don't worry, we're going!' laughed Asti through the door panel. 'We're going to look for some FLEA POWDER!' she shrieked.

Nelly turned towards Freeb and smiled. 'Take no notice of them, Freeby.'

'What's fleas, Nelly?' asked Freeb innocently.

'Nothing for you to worry about,' said Nelly.

Freeb held Marvin out with her arms and then pressed him to her red, furry cheek.

'GRUB'S UP!' shouted Nelly's dad from the patio. 'COME AND GET IT!'

Nelly held out her hand. 'Would you like Marvin to be your special guest at the barbecue, Freeby? He can sit on your lap if you like.'

Freeb nodded and placed her paw inside Nelly's hand.

'I like Marvin,' she growled. 'Does Marvin like me?'

'Marvin loves you,' smiled Nelly, leading Freeb to the top of the stairs.

'Do Asti and Natalie like me?' growled Freeb.

'Of course they do,' frowned Nelly.

8

When Nelly and Freeb arrived back at the barbecue they found that everyone had already begun to tuck in. Dad was cautiously sniffing a mungus steak, Mum was spooning mayonnaise on to a jacket potato and Asti and Natalie were sitting by the table with liberally-filled paper plates on their knees.

'Come and help yourself,' said Mum, directing Nelly to a banquet of barbecued nosh that Dad had tonged high on a large serving plate. 'Would you ask Freeb what she'd like to eat please, Nelly, and put some on a plate for her?'

'You're not putting *me* on a plate!' snorted Asti.

Nelly glared at her sister and then led Freeb over to the table.

'Come and help yourself,' said Mum.

'I'm strong,' said Freeb, lifting Marvin above
her head.

Asti pinched her nose like a clothes peg and then pointed at a wrought-iron chair with her foot.

'Nelly, you're sitting over here and Freeb, your place is over there,' she sniped, pointing at Snowball's cage. 'Ooops, sorry, Freeb, that's the rabbit cage, my mistake. All that fur got me confused.'

Natalie blurted a giggle and then went slightly red when she realised Asti's joke had landed like a lead balloon.

'Asti, can I have a word indoors a moment?' said her mum with a frown. Asti stood up, a picture of innocence, and carried her paper plate into the kitchen.

Two minutes later she returned, concealing her smirk behind a drumstick.

Nelly's mum threw a despairing look at her husband and then returned to the table in search of spring onions.

'These mungus steaks are delicious!' growled Clifford, working his teeth along one side of a large, lemon-coloured bone.

'Yes,' said Freeb, popping her steak in whole and bringing her higgledy-piggledy fangs together with a loud splintering crack.

Nelly's dad jumped and then peered uncertainly at his plate. 'You eat the bones then?' he said.

'Yes,' said Freeb. 'I eat my dinner all up like a good girl.'

Asti leaned sideways and drew her lips to Natalie's ear. 'You see what I mean. She could eat us all, and there wouldn't be a shred of evidence.'

Natalie brought her teeth together around a satay stick and shuddered.

'Would you like a sheep dip, I mean, another drink,' said Asti, looking sweetly at Freeb.

Freeb looked at her half-full glass of lemonade and then shook her head. 'No thank you very much, Asti,' she growled.

'Can *I* have a word with you indoors a minute, *please*!' growled Nelly, her toes curling so tight that they were almost touching her heels.

'I'm a bit busy at the moment,' said Asti, casually decapitating a jumbo Atlantic prawn.

'*Now!*' glared Nelly, piercing Asti's forehead with a skewer-sharp stare.

Asti rolled her eyes melodramatically, scraped some prawns eggs on to the side of her plate with her finger and slowly stood up.

'If you must then,' she said, 'but be quick, my lettuce is getting cold.'

Nelly stood up from her chair and marched into the kitchen. 'I won't be a minute, Freeb,' she said.

Asti sighed, handed her plate to Natalie and followed Nelly indoors.

'What the hell do you think you're playing at?' snapped Nelly, trying her best not to be heard over 'The Birdy Song'.

Asti folded her arms and shook her head. 'I'm sure I haven't the slightest clue what you mean,' she lied.

'You've been rude to Freeb from the very moment she arrived,' glared Nelly, 'that's what I mean!'

'Have I?' sighed Asti. 'Oh dear, I didn't mean to be rude, sis, it's just that I've never shared my birthday with a one-eyed carpet before.'

'There you go again!' growled Nelly.

'Ooops,' said Asti.

'Well it better stop right now or . . .' stammered Nelly.

'Or what?' yawned Asti.

'Or . . . *Or!* That's what!' fumed Nelly.

'Can I go now?' sighed Asti.

'Yes!' snapped Nelly.

'So kind,' sneered Asti.

The two sisters returned to the patio and rejoined their separate camps.

The next ten minutes of munches and crunches were conducted in a somewhat frosty silence. Freeb tucked in with the appetite of a lion, Nelly's mum declared the nut burgers an unqualified success, the girls picked and mixed and nibbled and chewed most of what was on offer and Snowball just sat back with floppy-eared gratitude as a mountain of salad was pressed through the wire of his cage by a new, equally hairy friend.

With his plate littered with mungus bones and his primeval lust for full-on meat satisfied at last, Nelly's dad switched his attention to the jov cheeks.

'I'll clear some stuff away while you swat the wasps,' smiled Nelly's mum, collecting the paper plates from the girls' laps and dumping them into a bin bag that she had ready beside the door.

'I'm strong,' growled Freeb, scampering across the patio with the tomato ketchup bottle held high above her head.

'Change the record,' yawned Asti.

As predicted, the jov cheeks drew a hangar full of fresh wasps into the garden but as they buzzed greedily around the end of the skewers they were sucked into oblivion by the geronimoniums. In contrast to the wasps, Asti and Natalie kept their distance from the Huffaluks' dessert, preferring vanilla ice cream to 'poisonous muck'.

Freeb, Nelly and her dad proved big fans though, and it was a full twenty minutes before the last jov cheek had been roasted, the last wasp munched, and the last finger licked, licked and licked.

'A success, I think!' said Nelly's dad, leaning back in his chair and unbuttoning the top button of his jeans. 'Our best barbecue yet, I believe!'

'HAS ANYONE SEEN THE SCOURING PAD?' shouted Mum from the kitchen.

'It's talking to Nelly!' sniggered Asti, throwing a contemptuous look at Freeb.

Natalie snorted her lemonade out through her nose and began dabbing apologetically at her blouse.

'Shut it!' mouthed Nelly.

'Ooops!' mouthed Asti.

'What's that, Nelly?' said Freeb, pointing to the end of the garden with three paws and a teddy.

Nelly turned and smiled. 'It's a swing, Freeb. Asti and I have had it since we were little girls like you. Would you and Marvin like to have a go?'

Freeb nodded her head enthusiastically.

'Mind you don't fall off, Freeb, we don't want to have to take you to the vet's.'

'ASTI!' said her dad, who had just about had enough of her rudeness.

'Ooops again,' smirked Asti.

Nelly took Freeb by the paw and led her down the garden.

'Mind it doesn't buckle under the weight!' shouted Asti. 'Oops – I did it again,' she cackled.

'Asti's funny, isn't she?' growled Freeb, pressing Nelly's teddy against her cheek again.

'She'd be *dead* funny if I had my way,' muttered Nelly.

Nelly had a fond spot for the garden swing. Although she and Asti had really outgrown it, she had so many happy memories of swinging to and fro and hanging upside down from the frame and staring at the house that she simply couldn't bear to have it dismantled. Her dad was keen for it to make way for a new vegetable patch, but so far Nelly had managed to thwart his every attempt. Nelly and her swing were old friends and so, she was determined, they would remain.

'This is what you do, Freeb,' said Nelly, placing her bottom on the faded blue rubber seat and closing her palms tightly around each chain.

With a little kick of her legs she set the swing in motion.

Freeb watched with growing interest as Nelly soared gradually higher.

'Me now, Nelly, me now!' she stomped.

Nelly laughed and then applied the brakes with the toes of her trainers. 'OK, Freeb. I can see you've got the idea of it.'

Nelly slid off the swing seat and helped Freeb lift her red, furry bottom into place.

'Now then,' said Nelly, adopting the role of Swing Commander General. 'Hold Marvin with your middle paw and these chains with your outer paws. That's right. Now you sit tight and I'm going to go behind you and push.'

Freeb gripped Marvin and the chains tightly and waited breathlessly for the next exciting instalment.

'Here we go,' said Nelly, placing her fingers gently on to the little Huffaluk's furry, red shoulders and pushing her gently in the direction of the house.

A smile as broad as a coathanger broke across Freeb's face as her feet and bottom were set in motion.

'Again!' she growled. 'Again, Nelly, again.'

Nelly looked over Freeb's shoulders towards the patio. Her mum and dad were standing by the kitchen door, waving encouragement. Asti and Natalie were practising their scowls.

'Now me push,' growled Freeb. 'Now me push Nelly. I'm strong.'

'MAKE SURE YOU DISINFECT THE SEAT!' screeched Asti, folding like a pasting table into a fit of sniggers and snorts.

Nelly pretended not to hear her and held the chains steady while Freeb jumped down.

'Okey dokey, Freeby, your turn to push,' said Nelly, swapping places and waiting patiently for Freeb and Marvin to toddle round behind her.

With a growl of excitement, Freeb placed two paws flat against the seat and nudged Nelly gently in the direction of the patio.

'I'm strong, Nelly,' growled Freeb.

'I know you are,' smiled Nelly, pushing her toes into the ground to give Freeb a little extra nudge in the right direction.

'I'm strong, Marvin,' said Freeb, pressing the teddy to her cheek.

'Freeb is very strong, Marvin,' smiled Nelly.

'Me now again,' growled Freeb, toddling round to face Nelly and pointing at the seat.

'OK, Freeb!' laughed Nelly. 'My turn to push again!'

Nelly helped Freeb and her teddy into position on the seat once more and then returned to her role of pusher. Freeb loved it. And so, apparently, did Marvin.

'Tell me if it's too high!' said Nelly, conscious not to push too hard. Freeb kicked her feet, settling for the easy sway of a clock pendulum.

'Me push now, Nelly!' she growled again.

Once again they swapped roles from pusher to swinger and from swinger to pusher.

Nelly was just about to take Marvin for a ride herself, when a shout from Asti halted proceedings.

'YOUR PHONE'S RINGING, NELLSMELL!' she squawked.

Nelly dug her toes into the earth and turned towards her sister.

'YOUR FREAK PHONE IS RINGING IN YOUR BEDROOM! HURRY UP OR YOU'LL MISS IT!'

Nelly looked up at her bedroom window. She couldn't hear her phone ringing but then her windows were closed and her dad's 80s chart blockbusters weren't helping either.

She turned to Freeb and placed Marvin in her middle paw. 'Look after Marvin for me a moment, Freeby,' she said. 'I've just got to run to answer my phone!'

'All right, Nelly,' growled Freeb, returning Marvin to her cheek.

Freeb waited by the swing seat as Nelly hurtled

down the lawn, leaped the patio with one bound and dived into the house through the kitchen doors.

'Look after Freeb,' she shouted as she hurtled towards the stairs.

Nelly's mum and dad craned their head around the kitchen door and threw warm, sunny smiles in the direction of the swing. With a wave of rubber gloves and a squeak of tea towels they returned to the washing-up.

Asti turned to Natalie and smiled with the menacing grin of a hyena.

'Fun time,' she purred.

With the merciless stares of two gunfighters, Asti and Natalie rose from their seats and strode menacingly in the direction of Freeb.

Freeb was standing behind the swing and trying her very best to balance Marvin on the seat.

'Outta the way, dog breath,' snarled Asti, towering over the toddler with a glowering stare. 'Outta the way of MY swing NOW or the teddy gets barbecued.'

With a frightened blink, Freeb stepped back from the swing and gripped Marvin with all three arms.

'How DARE you come to my house with your disgusting, ugly parents. How DARE you bring your flea-ridden fur into my presence and HOW DARE YOU bring your disgusting, maggot-infested food and put it anywhere NEAR our paper plates.

You leave me no choice but to make you my slave. Do you understand? From now on you are MY SLAVE and you will do everything that I ask. DO YOU HEAR ME? EVERYTHING I ASK!'

Freeb gripped Marvin tighter and nodded nervously at the two girls.

'NOW PUSH ME ON MY SWING, SLAVE! PUSH ME RIGHT NOW!'

Freeb scuttled round to the back of the swing as Asti eased her bum into place.

'Now push!' hissed Asti.

Quickly putting Marvin down, Freeb jumped nervously forward and tapped the back of the swing with her paws.

'HARDER!' snapped Asti.

Freeb looked anxiously at Natalie and then darted forward with another push.

Asti turned and leered at Natalie with a demonic wink.

'COME ON, YOU HAIRY WRETCH! DO YOU WANT TO SEE TEDDY IN FLAMES OR ARE YOU GOING TO OBEY MY COMMANDS? NOW,

FOR THE LAST TIME, **PUSH ME HARDER**! GIVE ME **EVERYTHING** THAT YOU'VE GOT!'

Nelly stepped out of the kitchen, her blood boiling. There hadn't been a call on her monster-sitting phone at all. Asti had made it up. She had just about had enough of her sister and was going to give her a piece of her mind.

But Asti was nowhere to be seen. She could see Freeb and Natalie and her mum and dad standing by the swing, but Asti had totally vanished.

'HEEEEEEEEEEEEEELLLLLLLLLPPP!' screeched Asti.

'Oops,' growled Freeb.

Nelly wheeled round and stared up at the roof. Asti was perched on the apex of the house with her arms and legs straddling the chimney stack.

'Get me down RIGHT NOW. That filthy hairy little fleabag pushed me up here,' she squealed.

'Sorry, Nelly' whispered Freeb. 'I pushed too hard.'

Asti was perched on the apex of the house with her
arms and legs straddling the chimney stack.

'Freeb is strong,' echoed Natalie, her eyes glued to the roof slates.

'What do you think we should do?' asked Nelly's dad trying his best to suppress a smile.

'Call a fire engine?' suggested Natalie.

'Leave her up there?' suggested Nelly.

Nelly's dad rested his chin in his hands. 'Well, Asti hasn't exactly been on her best behaviour today, has she?'

Nelly's mum shook her head slowly and then ran her fingers affectionately though Freeb's fur. 'Can anyone remember the number of the emergency services?'

'Oops! I've forgotten it!' smiled Nelly.

'Oops! I've forgotten it too!' smiled her mum.

Everyone looked at Marvin. But he had forgotten it as well.

'Never mind,' smiled Dad, taking Freeb by the paw. 'I'm sure it will come back to us later. Come on everybody, let's go and have some birthday fun!'

Freeb placed her other paw in Nelly's hand. 'I'm strong,' she growled.

'You certainly are!' laughed Nelly. 'If only we'd asked your daddy to push Asti on the swing, we could have sent her to the moon!'

The Muggots of Badley Hall

1

'Smile, Asti!' said Nelly, waving her hand in front of her sister's face but struggling to find a good angle.

'Smile, Snowball!' she said, thrusting her hand up to the wire mesh of the rabbit hutch.

'Smile, spotty wallpaper!' she said, turning her attentions to her bedroom wall.

'Smile, Mum'; 'Smile, Dad'; 'Smile, armchair'; 'Smile, grass'; 'Smile, carpet'; 'Smile, cornflakes'; 'Smile, shoelace'!

'MUM!' protested Asti, with an indignant stomp of both feet. 'Will you tell Nelly to stop taking photos with that stupid phone, she's driving me potty!'

Picture messaging had come to 66 Sweet Street. Nelly had pooled her birthday money and pocket

money and invested it in a new mobile phone. It was the very latest, totally coolest, Asti-hasn't-got-one model.

'Smile, Gorilla,' said Nelly, pointing her phone at Asti's face again and clicking the button provocatively with her thumb.

'I think I'll send this to Sergeant Shrew,' said Nelly. 'He can add it to his criminal files!'

'MUUUUMMM!' said Asti. 'Tell her!'

Nelly's mum lifted her eyes from the novel she was reading, and sighed. 'Nelly, will you stop waving that thing at everyone, or your dad will take it back to the shop.'

Nelly's dad prised his eyes away from the *Holiday* programme and looked at his wife. 'Why me?' he asked.

'Because, Clifford, I drove to the shop with Nelly to buy it. Therefore it will be your turn to drive to the shop if it has to go back. And anyway I'm right in the middle of my book at the moment,' she said, disappearing behind the pages.

Nelly's dad sat motionless in his favourite armchair and tried to fathom his wife's logic. Let's see, he was the only one in the Morton household that wasn't into mobile phones at all, in fact it was all he could do to remember his own number. He didn't know how to text, he hated the sound of the ring tone and was always forgetting to charge it. How then could he possibly be given the responsibility of returning a mobile phone to a shop? He shook his head in bewilderment and returned to the telly.

Nelly smiled. There were lots of places her mobile phone would be going, and back to the shop wasn't one of them. She slid the phone behind her back and took a random shot of the bookshelf.

'She did it again!' cried Asti, watching Nelly like a hawk. 'And she was doing it all last night in bed!' she blurted.

Nelly's mum peered over the book cover again and arched her eyebrows.

'I hope you weren't, young girl,' she glowered.

'She was!' said Asti. 'She had her phone in bed and she was sending pictures to all her friends until really late. And they were sending photos back!'

Nelly's mum placed the novel on her knee and iced Nelly with a stare.

'I wasn't!' fibbed Nelly, managing to keep her lips unfrozen. 'And anyway . . . how would Asti know what I was doing in my bedroom really late? UNLESS . . . she had come out of her own bedroom REALLY LATE to see!'

Nelly threw a triumphant look at Asti and waited to see how she would wriggle out of that one.

Asti's eyes danced like a gnat, before delivering a quick-fire but slow-witted response.

'I could hear the pictures,' she said, unconvincingly.

Nelly threw her arms in the air and began to bray like a donkey. 'Hear the pictures? You can't hear pictures!'

Nelly's mum cocked her head to one side and waited for another dubious explanation.

'You can if there's sound on them,' countered Asti, clutching at straws.

'Not from two bedrooms away!' laughed Nelly. 'And anyway I was doing it under the covers so there's no way anyone would have heard . . .'

Nelly's voice trailed into silence as she realised the admission she had just made.

'Hah!' said Asti, pouncing on her error like a cheetah. 'I told you so! She WAS sending pictures to all her friends REALLY LATE and she's just admitted it!'

Nelly had two choices. Fib again or take the rap. She wisely chose the latter.

'Clifford? Did you hear that? Your daughter has been picture messaging into the early hours when she should be tucked up asleep.'

Nelly's dad dragged his eyes reluctantly from the bikinis on the beach and prepared to endure a conversation involving phone technology.

'Picture whattaging?' he asked.

'Picture *messaging* . . . into the early hours! The VERY early hours, knowing your daughter.'

Nelly was always her dad's daughter when she had done something wrong.

'It wasn't that late!' protested Nelly. 'And anyway, Chloe wanted to show me her new trainers, and Marina's dog is about to have puppies and Holly's sister has just got her first love bite! Right there, it is,' elaborated Nelly, pointing to the side of her neck. 'It looks like a vampire's been sucking her blood!'

'I don't want to know, thank you,' shuddered Mum. 'Clifford, what are you going to do about it?'

A slightly hot feeling began to creep around the inside of Nelly's dad's shirt collar as the pressure to adjudicate on this matter began to build.

'I'm "pay as you go",' said Nelly, 'so I'm not costing you any more money.'

Nelly's dad didn't understand the first half of the sentence but was pleasantly reassured by the sound of the second half.

'Growing girls need their sleep,' countered her mum sternly.

'And don't forget that the late-night gamma waves from Nelly's phone could give us all cancer because your body's immune system is always at its lowest at night when you're asleep,' said Asti, who was clearly pressing for a life sentence.

Dad flicked his eyes back to the bikinis. If he wasn't careful, he was going to miss the *Tuscan Villa Special*. With a cough and a frown, he delivered his verdict.

'A phone curfew,' he pronounced. 'That's what we'll have. No more phoning or picture thingying after nine o'clock at night.'

'Not including emergencies,' said Nelly.

'Very well – not including emergencies,' conceded her dad. 'But no arguments. No discussions. My decision is final and the curfew includes your mobile too, Asti.'

Nelly looked relieved. At least she hadn't had her phone confiscated. Asti looked kneecapped. Why should she be punished for something her sister had done? And how could she possibly have her own midnight chats with Natalie Dupre if her own mobile was now out of action? The only person who looked pleased was Mum. In fact she looked more than pleased. Even impressed.

'You're so masterful sometimes, Clifford,' she purred, before slinking back into her book.

Dad puffed out his chest, sucked in his waist and joined the TV presenter in the foaming Tuscan surf.

2

'Smile, Grerk!' said Nelly, holding her phone over a page of her *Secret Monster-sitting Notebook*. She had decided to retire to her bedroom and transfer some useful monster-sitting info into her new phone. Her sketches, notes and telephone numbers would all be at her instant disposal from now on.

'Now I can keep all my monster friends on phone file!' she beamed, turning to the Squiddls on the next page. She positioned her phone carefully over her sketch of the Squiddl triplets at number 2 and clicked. There were lots of tentacles to get in. Too many, in fact.

'I'll delete that picture,' she murmured, 'and just go for a single shot. Actually, it's probably easier if I leave the leg tentacles out. Or maybe not?'

Her hand was hovering indecisively over the Squiddls when her attention was drawn to her locked bedroom door. Someone was knocking softly.

'Who is it?' said Nelly, already sure of the answer.

'It's me,' said Asti.

'Me who?' said Nelly.

'Asti,' said Asti.

'Asti who?' smiled Nelly.

'Look – let me in, will you?' sighed Asti.

'Look – let me in, will you who?' said Nelly, pushing the tease to breaking point.

'OK, if that's the way you want it, fine – don't use your phone after nine o'clock, see if I care,' said Asti.

Nelly slid her notebook under her bed, climbed to her knees quickly and skipped to the door. She turned the key slowly and peered suspiciously out into the hall. Asti was hovering outside with a 'deal-making' expression on her face.

'Can I come in?' she whispered. 'We don't want Mum and Dad to hear.'

Nelly nodded, and stepped to one side.

'OK,' said Asti, in the hushed tones of a gangster in a library, 'you want to use your phone under the covers at night and so do I, agreed?'

'Agreed,' said Nelly.

'So I have a proposal for you,' whispered Asti.

Nelly stayed quiet and allowed her sister to continue.

'My proposal is that we call a phone truce. You can use your phone under the covers at night and I won't split on you, and I can do the same but you won't split on me.'

'But you already have split on me,' said Nelly.

'That was then. I'm talking about from now on,' said Asti, brushing that little technicality under the carpet. 'From now on I won't split on you, and you won't split on me. What do you say?'

Nelly looked at her phone.

'Smile,' she said, thrusting it a centimetre from Asti's nose and clicking. 'You've got yourself a deal.'

Asti leaned backwards and waved the phone

away. 'I wish you'd stop doing that!' she protested.
'It's so annoying.'

'Smile again!' said Nelly, snapping once more
for luck.

Asti's temper frayed. She lashed out with her
hand and tried to wrestle the phone from Nelly's
grasp, but as she did so Nelly wrenched it back
and placed it to her ear.

'Hello?' Nelly said, wheeling round to protect
her phone from further assault.

The phone was ringing.

'Hello?' said Nelly.

But no one was there.

'Wrong phone, duuurrr brain,' said Asti, pointing to the table beside Nelly's bed.

Asti was right. It wasn't Nelly's new mobile that was ringing, it was her monster-sitting telephone. Nelly shoved her mobile into her pocket and dived across the room.

'Hello!' she gasped, snatching up the phone on the sixth ring. 'Nelly the Monster Sitter here!' The phone slid off the table and clattered on to the carpet, sending tremors up the spirals of the phone cord.

There was a pause.

There was a 'Gullop'.

And then there was a 'Hello'.

'Hello!' said Nelly, with a little more composure this time. 'Sorry about that, I dropped the phone!'

'Are you Nelly the Monster Sitter?' enquired the monster on the other end of the phone.

'That's me!' said Nelly, turning to Asti and

waving her out of the room. 'How can I help?'

'Do you monster sit Muggots?' gulloped the voice.

'I monster sit every type of monster!' said Nelly, motioning to Asti with her eyebrows to close the door behind her. Asti obliged with a grimace and a shudder.

'We're the Muggots of Badley Hall,' gulloped the monster. 'Do you know us?'

Nelly gasped.

'I know Badley Hall!' she said, sitting down on the bed. 'Everyone knows Badley Hall. It's the big house on the hill, behind the iron gates,' she said, choosing her words very carefully.

Badley Hall was indeed a very big house, a mansion in fact, located on the hill overlooking the town. But it was a house around which gossip and rumour abounded. Despite its prominent position, no one in the town had ever seen a single occupant inhabit the hall or grounds. Nelly's friends were convinced it was haunted.

'That's right,' gulloped the Muggot. 'We're on the hill, about three-quarters of a mile past the church.'

Nelly poked out her foot and slid her secret notebook out from under the bed.

'I'd be delighted to come and monster sit for you,' smiled Nelly, with an almost uncontrollable surge of excitement. 'When would you like me to come?'

The Muggot at the other end of the phone

drawled slightly and then cleared his throat with a gurgle.

'Would next Saturday be convenient?' he gulloped again. 'We have a bridge party to attend. Next Saturday – seven till midnight?'

'Midnight!' gasped Nelly. A tingle of adrenaline fizzed through her veins at the thought of monster sitting in a haunted house until the witching hour! 'I'll need special permission from my mum and dad if I'm going to stay out that late,' she explained.

'Would you like me to talk to your parents?' asked the Muggot with a snort and a gullop. 'I'd be happy to reassure them.'

Nelly shook her head and smiled. 'No, it's OK, I'll ask them myself,' she said, mindful that the throaty gullops of a Muggot might spoil her chances altogether. 'Why don't you give me your number and I'll call you back,' said Nelly.

'There's four of us,' gulloped the Muggot. 'My wife Agar, my two young children, Riggll and Rythe, and I.'

'I meant *telephone* number,' said Nelly.

'Oh, I see! Of course, I do beg one's pardon,' gulloped the Muggot. 'One misunderstood!'

As Nelly's strawberry gel-pen jotted the digits of the Muggots' phone number into her diary, she couldn't help thinking that she was going up in the world. Not only was Badley Hall on a hill, the Badley Hall Muggot was quite the poshest-sounding monster she had ever spoken to.

When she replaced the phone, she wasn't quite sure which way to turn first. Did she start a new page in her secret notebook or did she go straight downstairs and start working on her mum and dad? She'd never monster sat anywhere until midnight before. What were her parents going to say?

3

'No' was the answer.

'Midnight is too late' was the reason.

'But it's Saturday!' protested Nelly. 'I haven't got school in the morning and I'll make sure I do all my homework before I go out.'

'No,' said Mum firmly.

'I'm never asleep before midnight on a Saturday anyway,' protested Nelly.

'Yes, and we know why, don't we?' said Mum, throwing accusing glances at Nelly's phone.

Nelly swung her attentions towards the armchair.

'Dad, please let me monster sit until midnight. Just this once. Pleeeaaaassssse! I am twelve years old now.'

Nelly's dad pulled his eyes from the omnibus

edition of *Emergency Drainblock Ten* and whimpered at the thought of having to adjudicate twice in one day.

'What did your mum say?' he asked.

'She said to ask you,' fibbed Nelly.

'I said *no*!' growled Mum, looking up sternly from the final chapter of her book.

'No it is, then,' said Dad, settling back to watch thirty drain rods assembled under sniper-fire conditions.

Nelly sidled over to the back of the armchair and slipped her arms around her dad's shoulders.

'I'll clean the car,' she whispered.

'We are not open to bribery, Petronella!' countered her mum.

'And I'll clean Snowball out.'

'It's your turn to clean Snowball out anyway,' said Asti, whose phone-truce agreement didn't extend to late pass negotiations.

Nelly's mum bobbed up from behind her book again and sighed. 'I don't know what's wrong with the youth of today. In my day, a "No" was a "No".'

'I'll wash up every day for a week,' said Nelly, trying to find a chink in her mum's armour.

Nelly's mum's shoulders twitched, and her eyebrows arched.

'And I'll do the ironing for a month,' said Nelly, playing her trump card.

There was a pause as Mum's fingers closed tightly on the cover of her novel and her eyes rooted to the page.

Nelly waited with baited breath.

Her mum's eyeballs had stuck in mid sentence and her body had turned stiller than a Madame Tussaud's waxwork.

'Actually, Clifford,' she said, suddenly breaking from her reverie, 'I don't think midnight is such a big issue. After all, it's another opportunity for Nelly to meet some new monsters and we know what a lovely time she has when she monster sits. What's a couple of hours extra here or there? As long as you're there to pick her up bang on the stroke of twelve, Clifford, I see no reason at all why Nelly shouldn't go.'

'Yesssssss!' cried Nelly, giving her dad a Huffaluk hug.

Nelly's dad's glasses skewed from his nose and the cesspit tanker he was watching disappeared from the TV screen in a blur.

'Why do I have to be the one who picks Nelly

up so late?' he moaned, a little aggrieved at being volunteered for taxi duties twice in one day.

'Well, you wouldn't want me driving through those rusty iron gates and down that long, dark, gravel drive to that huge, ghostly mansion all on my own at midnight, would you?' reasoned Nelly's mum.

'Of course not,' he mumbled. 'You might frighten the bats.'

Nelly burst out laughing and smiled broadly but briefly at her mum.

'Ironing, Miss Morton,' her mum frowned. 'There's a pile in the kitchen. You can make a start now.'

4

'Dad needs some new underpants!' shouted Nelly, trying to bring another faded pair of tatty boxer shorts back to life with the steam iron.

'Keep your voice down!' said her mum, closing the kitchen window. 'We don't want the whole world to know!'

'Too late!' said Nelly, using her new phone to despatch a photo of her dad's boxers to all her friends.

Nelly had been on ironing and tea-towel duties all week. Her mum had held her to her promise and had added emptying the dishwasher to her long list of jobs. And yet despite the acres of creases, collars and cuffs and the sink loads of dried-on scrambled egg, burnt sausage trays and cremated moussaka dishes, Nelly had gone about her duties with a smile and a click.

Whether she was stooping over the ironing board or up to her elbows in suds, her new phone was never far from her side. Not surprisingly for a girl of Nelly's imagination she had found creative photo opportunities almost everywhere she had looked. She had sent a picture text of a potato that looked like a willy to her best friends Marina and Chloe. She had compiled a photographic exhibition of her dad's shirt buttons, snapped all her mum's designer labels, got the entire contents of the fridge to 'exude' and done some really avant-garde work with the contents of the pedal bin.

'Will you put that phone down, Nelly,' said her mum, 'before I throw it in the wheelie bin.'

Nelly smiled, slipped the phone back into her pocket and cut an expert swathe along the sleeve of her sardine sweatshirt.

'Good as new!' she exclaimed, holding it up to inspect her handiwork.

'OK, you've persuaded me,' said Nelly's mum. 'You've got the job for life.'

Nelly shook her head and turned the steam iron off at the socket.

'No thanks,' she laughed. 'Three more weeks and I'm resigning. That was our deal.'

Nelly had never worked so hard for a late pass. She had been allowed to stay up past midnight on various occasions before, but never alone with monsters in a haunted house on a hill!

Nervous excitement was already beginning to bubble through her veins as she despatched the empty ironing basket into the kitchen cupboard and wound the iron cord tidily around her wrist. It was six-fifteen. She had twenty-five minutes to get ready. In just forty-five minutes she would knocking on the door of Badley Hall!

She had pictured the moment when the front door of Badley Hall would creak open, over and over again in her mind. She strongly fancied that the front porch would be covered in cobwebs and that a giant, oak-panelled door would squeak open with the low, creaking groan of a rusty coffin lid. One eye would probably greet her, pizza-sized and emerald green. And a long, bony finger with a dragon's claw fingernail would beckon her inside. At least that's what she reckoned. Would she be right? Would she be wrong? The answer was only forty-four minutes away now!

Nelly left the kitchen with her sardine sweatshirt folded neatly over her arm. As she walked past the lounge, she spotted her dad surfing the TV channels.

'It's nearly time to go!' she said, running up the stairs to her bedroom.

'What time have you ordered your taxi for?' smiled her dad.

'I've got a chauffeur booked for quarter to,' laughed Nelly.

When Nelly returned downstairs, her dad was waiting dutifully by the front door with the car keys in his hand.

'Where to, madam?' he asked with a bow.

'Badley Hall please, Jeeves,' smiled Nelly.

Nelly's dad opened the front door and then stepped courteously to one side to allow Nelly to leave the house first.

'Allow me,' he said, quickly overtaking her and hurrying around the Maestro to open Nelly's passenger door.

'Charmed, I'm sure,' said Nelly, sliding into her seat. 'Oh and Jeeves, may I just say how

particularly well-ironed your rugby shirt is this fine evening.'

'Why thank you, madam,' said her dad. 'We have a new slave girl working for us in the kitchen at present.'

'Please send her my regards,' smiled Nelly.

As the car pulled off the drive Nelly raised her phone to her eye and framed the view through the windscreen. 'Smile, Natalie,' she said, before deciding at the last moment not to waste a click on Asti's friend.

'Mum says I should come inside with you for a moment when we get there,' said her dad, 'just to make sure everything is OK.'

'Whatever,' Nelly smiled, directing her phone towards a dog that was cocking his leg up a lamppost on the corner of Peppermint Street.

'I'm going to send this one to Craig,' she smiled.

Ten minutes further down the road, Craig's picture text response arrived in the form of a piece of home-grown wildlife photography entitled '*Slug meets salt*'.

'What are you laughing at?' asked her dad.

'Nothing,' smiled Nelly, turning the screen away from view.

'I wish I had your head for technology,' said her dad, beginning the slow climb out of the Montelimar Estate and up Bootlace Hill. 'These new-fangled mobiles are gobbledygook to me.'

'It's easy when you get the hang of it,' said Nelly, looking eagerly ahead for a break in the tree line that fringed both sides of the hill. 'You just have to practise.'

'Your mum said the same thing about chopsticks,' said her dad. 'I still have to ask for a fork when we go to the Chinese.'

'There it is!' said Nelly, pressing her finger to the windscreen.

As the car levelled out at the top of Bootlace Hill, the line of mature beech trees petered out on the passenger side of the road and was replaced by an imposing grey stone wall.

'That's the wall outside Badley Hall,' said Nelly.

'I bet you could fit twenty cricket pitches inside that garden!'

Nelly's dad leaned forward and flicked his right-hand indicator. 'Oh look, there's been another accident,' he said, acknowledging the waves of a policeman standing in the middle of the road.

Nelly peered ahead. A Freshco's supermarket delivery van had skewed off the road ahead of them and narrowly missed crashing into the wall of Badley Hall.

Nelly's dad steered the Maestro slowly past the sweeping line of traffic cones and peered inside the back of the lorry.

'It's very strange, you know,' said Nelly's dad. 'This is a real accident black spot and yet it's such a straight stretch of road. It doesn't make sense at all.'

Nelly swung her eyes away from the deep furrows that had been gouged by the lorry's tyres into the grassy verge and looked excitedly ahead to the gates of the Badley Hall estate.

As the car began to slow, Nelly started to flap her hands manically.

'It's for sale!' exclaimed Nelly. 'Look – Badley Hall is up for sale!'

Sure enough, a wooden sign staked into the grass verge just outside the gated entrance confirmed that Badley Hall had recently been placed on the housing market.

Nelly's dad turned the car off the road and pulled up with the bumper facing the gate.

'Cool gargoyles!' said Nelly, peering up excitedly. 'Look – that one's got two tongues!'

Nelly's dad craned his eyes upwards to the top of the grey stone pillars that stood like giant sentries either side of the gate. Crouched on top of each pillar was an antlered slug with a broad, downturned mouth and staring bulbous eyes.

'I'm glad I haven't got any of those in the garden,' he shuddered. 'My lettuces wouldn't stand a chance.'

Nelly stared bulbously back at them and then began to comb the ivy-clad pillars with her eyes.

Crouched on top of each pillar was an
antlered slug with a broad downturned mouth
and staring bulbus eyes.

'How do we get in?' she said. 'Can you see any sign of a doorbell?'

Nelly's dad shook his head. 'There's probably an entry phone somewhere under the ivy. Big houses always have entry phones,' he said.

He placed his hand on his seat belt and prepared to undo the strap, but as his thumb slid over the button, Nelly began flapping her hands again.

'They're opening, Dad, look – they're opening!'

Nelly's dad leaned back in his seat and placed both hands on the steering wheel. Nelly was right. Without any prompting at all, the huge iron gates of Badley Hall had slowly begun to creak open.

5

'You bow, I'll curtsey,' said Nelly, as the car began its crunching, crumbling journey along the gravel drive towards the mansion.

'I beg your pardon?' exclaimed her dad.

'When we meet the Muggots, I'll curtsey and you bow. They're bound to be posh, living in a big house like this. It's important that we create the right impression.'

Nelly's dad nodded uncertainly and flicked his eyes at the driver's mirror. The gates behind them were automatically closing.

'I wonder why they want to move house?' said Nelly, a little disappointed that this might be her one and only visit.

'From the look of the grounds, I expect the grass takes too long to cut,' said her dad.

The gardens inside the wall were badly neglected. The lawns had become a savannah of chest-high grass, and even the weeds were choked with weeds.

'I see what you mean,' said Nelly. 'You'd never find a cricket ball in here!'

'You'd be hard pushed to find the pavilion!' said her dad.

'There's the house!' said Nelly, losing interest in her phone for the first time that week and stuffing it away into her pocket. 'Look – there it is, at the end of the driveway!'

Nelly's dad nodded and then peered at his petrol gauge.

'I might need to fill up with petrol just to get to the end of the drive!' he joked.

Nelly laughed and leaned forward in her seat.

'It's got turrets!' she said excitedly. 'It's got turrets on the roof just like a castle!'

Nelly swept her eyes left towards the bell tower; located centrally in one wing of the house and then right towards the clock tower; similarly positioned on the opposite wing.

'And look, the numbers on that clock go up to fourteen!' she gasped.

Badley Hall was drawing closer, looming large but mysteriously lifeless. Part mansion, part fortress, it was built in the Dracula style from blocks of sturdy grey granite. Faded with age but towering with presence, it reminded Nelly of a wedding cake that had stood uneaten for centuries.

Nelly peered up at the dark slitted windows, searching for signs of twitching curtains. But the heavy grey drapes that framed each pane hung drab and deathly still.

'I wonder if they've got a butler?' she asked. 'I wonder how many heads he'll have!'

Gravel pinged from the tyres, and dust from the long, sun-beaten driveway began to coat the bonnet of the car. Nelly wound down her window and leaned out for a better view.

'That's a strange bell tower!' said Nelly, shielding her eyes from the early evening sun and trying to make sense of a huge black shape that was suspended in silhouette against the blood-red skyline. Instead of swinging noisily like a bell, it was moving up and down silently like a yo-yo.

With a crunch of tyres and a squeak of the handbrake, Nelly's dad swung the Maestro around. They had pulled up at the foot of a monumentally steep flight of steps.

'Now that's what I call an entrance!' he said, peering up the steps to a pair of bright-red cathedral-style doors.

'Muggots, here we come!' chimed Nelly, unclipping her seat belt and climbing excitedly out of the car.

'Do I really have to bow when I meet them?' sighed her dad, closing the driver's door and joining Nelly at the foot of the steps.

'Yes,' said Nelly, with a little practice curtsey. 'I've already told you. First impressions are very important.'

Nelly linked her arm through her dad's and together they began climbing the stone steps.

'Couldn't I just shake their hands?' puffed her dad, taking a breather at step twelve.

'They might not have hands,' cautioned Nelly.

'Remind me never to take you to the pyramids,' gasped her dad, doubling over at step twenty-five. 'I think I'm getting a stitch.'

When he lifted his head he discovered that Nelly was no longer beside him. She had skipped from his side, sprung up the remaining steps and was standing with her nose just centimetres away from the Badley Hall front doors.

'Wait for me!' he wheezed.

'Weird,' Nelly murmured, stooping for a closer look. Both of the doors to Badley Hall appeared to be coated with red wax.

'It's like an Edam cheese,' she murmured, prodding the doors softly with her finger.

Even more intriguingly, the wax was etched with weird lettering, skulls, crossbones and even crucifix symbols. Nelly scratched her head and frowned. She felt sure they must be the mysterious runes and verses of an ancient monster tongue.

'They're gravestone prints,' gulloped a snorting, snuffling voice from behind them. 'One had them specially done.'

Nelly and her dad spun round and their eyes tumbled thirty steps back down on to the gravel drive. The Muggots of Badley Hall were standing in a group beside the Maestro, peering up at them with pale, milky eyes.

'You're supposed to bow, not curtsey!' whispered Nelly as her dad's knees folded beneath him.

'Sorry,' he whispered back. 'They took me by surprise!'

'Me too,' whispered Nelly, coming out of her own curtsey with a smile and a wave.

'I'm Nelly the Monster Sitter,' she called, walking with as much poise as she could back down the steps. 'It's a pleasure and an honour to meet you.'

'Hear hear!' said her dad, with a puff and a stumble. 'Morton, Clifford T. Morton. So awfully pleased to make one's acquaintance, your very highnesses.'

'Don't overdo it,' whispered Nelly. 'It's Badley Hall, not Buckingham Palace.'

'Sorry,' whispered her dad through clenched teeth. 'I've never met a Right Honourable Monster before.'

Nelly offered her dad her arm and helped him negotiate the remaining steps down to Muggot level.

'Let me do the talking,' she whispered, extending a friendly hand to the principal

Muggot who was standing slightly forward of the others, sporting a yellow and green polka-dot cravat.

'Hello again,' she smiled politely. 'We were just admiring your front door.'

'Damn thing,' snuffled the Muggot. 'I wish I'd never had it dipped. Haven't been able to open them since. Darned things keep sticking.'

'That's why it took us so long to greet you,' said the Muggot standing next to him, tinkering with her necklace of barbed wire and pearls. 'We've had to walk right round from the tradesmen's

entrance in the east wing. So sorry for the delay. It really is a pleasure to meet you, Nelly. An absolute pleasure.'

'This is my dad,' smiled Nelly. 'He gave me a lift over here.'

The Muggots turned to Nelly's dad and extended their long, scimitar-shaped pincers towards him.

Nelly's dad held out his hand anxiously and then withdrew it sharply for fear of losing his fingers.

'He's a bit nervous,' apologised Nelly.

'We understand,' smiled the cravatted Muggot. 'Allow me to make some formal introductions.'

Nelly's dad's eyes kept a close watch on the pincers as the Muggot waved his arm.

'My name is Leafmould. We're the twelfth generation of Leafmoulds to live in this house,' he gulloped proudly. 'Permit me to introduce you to my family.'

Nelly tugged her dad by the sleeve and led him along the line of smiling Muggots. They were like giant wasp grubs, with pulsating white bodies of pale, rubbery skin covered in soft, cactus-like hairs. Their heads were smooth and shiny and their dainty, buttermilk eyes were shaped like upside-down tear drops.

'Allow me to present my wife, Agar,' the Muggot snuffled proudly, tapping his wife tenderly on the shoulder with the tip of a pincer.

The armoured shell of Agar's beetle-like legs folded with a squeak and as she curtsied her body rippled like a caterpillar.

'Charmed, I'm sure,' she gulloped.

Nelly's dad managed a flicker of a smile and then swallowed hard as they progressed along the line to the children.

'And these are my sons and heirs,' snuffled Leafmould proudly.

'You must be Riggll and Rythe,' smiled Nelly with a wink. 'Are you ready to have some fun later?'

The thin green lips of the Muggot brothers broke into broad, runner-bean smiles.

'Not half!' they snuffled and snorted.

'Say hello to Riggll and Rythe,' whispered Nelly, tugging her dad on the sleeve.

Nelly's dad's lips parted almost imperceptibly. 'Hello's were the last thing on his mind. It wasn't the Muggot children's pincers that had his undivided attention now, it was their shoulders. Or rather the vicinity of their shoulders.

Nelly tugged his sleeve again, but her dad was transfixed with fear.

She followed the javelined path of his gaze and then squealed.

'There's a hedgehog on your shoulder, Riggll!' she gasped. 'And yours!' she screamed, pointing to Rythe.

The two Muggot brothers looked at each other and started to snort uncontrollably.

'They're not hedgehogs!' they snuffled. 'Haven't you seen a spider before?'

Nelly's eyes split in two different directions at once and telescoped towards the creatures that were perched like parrots on both the brothers' shoulders.

'They can't be spiders, they're huge!' she gasped.

'They're only babies,' laughed Rythe, holding his left pincer up to his shoulder and coaxing the spider on to his claw. 'Their mum's a gigantula. She lives in the old bell tower.'

Nelly peered up at the giant yo-yo silhouetted in the bell tower and gulped. So that's what it was!

'I don't like spiders,' whispered Nelly's dad, limping one step backwards towards the car.

'You can hold him if you like,' said Rythe.

Nelly stepped forward and held out both hands.

'I don't like spiders,' whispered her dad again, two limps further away now.

Rythe shooed the spider from the tip of his pincer and shepherded it into Nelly's palms.

'It's like a coconut on legs!' laughed Nelly, paddling her hands through the air as the giant spider tried to make progress up the arm of her sweatshirt.

'I don't like spiders,' whimpered her dad, reaching into his pocket for his car keys.

Leafmould and Agar watched in astonishment

as Nelly's dad limped further and further back towards the Maestro.

'Wouldn't you care to come into the house for a glass of refreshment?' asked Leafmould.

'I don't like spiders,' murmured Nelly's dad.

'He doesn't like spiders,' explained Nelly, placing her eight-legged coconut back on to Rythe's shoulder and sidling over to the car.

'I don't like spiders,' mumbled her dad, fumbling for the keyhole.

'I know you don't like spiders,' said Nelly, 'but if you want to come into the Hall and take a look around, don't you think you're walking the wrong way?'

'I don't like spiders,' muttered her dad.

Nelly looked back at the Muggots and waved politely. 'I'm afraid my dad needs to take leave of us. He has a prior engagement!'

The Muggots waved back politely.

'I'll see you at midnight then,' whispered Nelly, kissing her dad on the cheek.

'I'm not coming in,' he murmured. 'I'm not

going anywhere near those spiders. I'll wait for you on the drive.'

'But how will I know you've arrived?' whispered Nelly.

'I'll ring you on your mobile,' whispered her dad.

'What? After nine o'clock?' grinned Nelly. 'Whatever happened to your curfew?'

'I'm an emergency,' whispered her dad.

Nelly watched as her dad climbed shakily into the Maestro, and immediately activated the central locking on all four doors. With the windows closed tight and the car spider-proofed he turned the key in the ignition and pointed the dusty bonnet back in the direction of the gates.

'See you later,' mouthed Nelly through the windscreen.

With a wide-eyed stare Nelly's dad put his foot down and wheel-spun the Maestro down the drive.

Nelly waved until the car was out of sight and then turned to the Muggots with a smile.

'He really doesn't like spiders,' she explained.

6

It was a very, very long walk back to the east wing. Not only was the tradesmen's entrance located at the very, very back of the building, but the single-file track through the jungle of weeds and tall grass made progress along the flanks of the Hall even slower. Despite the ever-present stingers and prickles, Nelly wasted no time acquainting herself with Riggll and Rythe, taking each Muggot by the pincer and turning sideways like a Greek dancer to negotiate the narrow path through the weeds.

'I notice that you've put Badley Hall up for sale,' said Nelly, throwing her voice to the head of the line. 'Where will you go?'

'Somewhere scarier,' gurgled Leafmould, shearing a clump of thistles with his pincer. 'We need to find somewhere scarier to live, for the sake of the children.'

Nelly shook her head and squeezed gingerly past a huge bank of stinging nettles that flanked the southern wall. Had she heard Leafmould correctly? Agar confirmed that she had.

'Yes, we've tried our best to make our home as frightening as possible, but we're fighting a losing battle, I'm afraid.'

'It looks pretty scary to me!' Nelly said, peering uncomfortably at an assortment of hangman's nooses that were suspended from the gnarled branches of the overgrown Badley Hall orchard.

'Oh, take no notice of those,' said Agar, dismissing the nooses with a wave of her largest pincer. 'We put those there to spook the children when they were babies, but they didn't work either.'

'Just like the bally front doors,' grumbled Leafmould. 'All that expense dipping them in blood-red wax, not to mention the dashed trouble of lifting the gravestones from the family graveyard.'

'We had the gravestones pressed into the wax . . .' explained Agar.

'To make scary imprints in the front door,' continued Leafmould.

'But when we showed them to the children . . .'

'They just laughed,' gurgled Leafmould.

'Hardly surprising,' grumbled Agar. 'All the lettering came out back to front.'

'We're not frightened of anything!' gurgled Riggll proudly.

'We can't go to sleep unless we're frightened,' explained Rythe.

'It's a family curse,' sighed Leafmould.

Nelly walked on in confused silence for a moment. Were her ears deceiving her? Were Leafmould and Agar genuinely trying to *frighten* their children to sleep? She was intrigued. She was more than intrigued. She let go of Riggll and Rythe's pincers and ran to catch up with Leafmould.

'Please tell me more!' she whispered to Leafmould. 'Maybe I can help!'

Leafmould smiled appreciatively but shook his head with proud resignation. 'Many have tried. All have failed,' he grunted.

'Try me anyway,' said Nelly, always one to welcome a challenge.

'One really doesn't wish to burden you with our problems,' he said, batting away another batch of thistles.

Nelly liked problems. Especially monster problems. She darted ahead of Leafmould, turned and blocked his path.

'I insist!' said Nelly, looking determinedly into Leafmould's aristocratic eyes.

Leafmould lurched to a halt, toyed with his cravat for a moment and then turned to his wife with a frown.

Agar placed her pincers on the boys' shoulders and gave them a consoling hug. 'We appreciate your concern, Nelly, but there really is nothing that can be done.'

Nelly folded her arms stubbornly and refused to budge.

'Very well, young Nelly,' smiled Leafmould. 'I will tell you everything, but on one condition only. That you join us for a glass of demonade before Agar and I leave for our bridge party!'

'I can't think of anything I'd like better!' laughed Nelly, hooking her arm through Leafmould's pincer and allowing him to escort her indoors.

'Welcome to Badley Hall,' said Leafmould, stamping his feet on an 'Unwelcome' mat that lay on the scuffed floor of the tradesmen's entrance.

'This didn't scare us either,' laughed Riggll, as he wiped his feet.

7

'Riggll and Rythe haven't slept one wink since the day they were born,' gurgled Leafmould.

'What – not once?' gasped Nelly.

'Not once,' sighed Agar.

'What – never ever?' gulped Nelly.

'Never ever,' sighed Leafmould.

'Eight years, seven months and twelve nights precisely,' said Agar, decanting a glass of demonade into a lead crystal goblet.

'That's terrible,' said Nelly, raising the goblet to her lips. 'Not the demonade I mean – the demonade is delicious!' she said, gulping down the purple, frothy liquid. 'No, I meant it's terrible that Riggll and Rythe have never once been to sleep in all those years!'

Leafmould placed his pincer on the

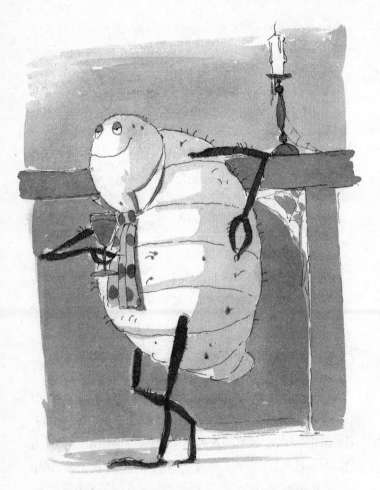

*Leafmould placed his pincer on the mantelpiece of
the drawing room, crossed his legs and struck up
the pose of an English country gentleman.*

mantelpiece of the drawing room, crossed his legs and struck up the pose of an English country gentleman. 'We knew what you meant, Nelly,' he smiled. 'Would you like some more?'

Nelly held out her goblet and Agar stepped forward to top her up.

'Aren't they tired?' Nelly whispered, nodding across the crimson rug towards the brothers, who were playing by the window. 'I'd be exhausted if I hadn't had any sleep for eight years!'

'It's all they've ever known,' said Agar. 'Sleep is just something they've become used to not having.'

Nelly's mind began to tick over. She raised the goblet of demonade to her lips and furrowed her brow.

'And is it true what Riggll said? That Muggots have to be frightened before they can get to sleep?' she asked.

'Muggots with Neinschnoozen Syndrome, yes,' explained Leafmould.

Nelly snorted into her demonade and her eyes

began to water as the bubbles fizzed up her nose.

'I do beg your pardon,' she spluttered, wiping her mouth with her sleeve. 'What did you say?'

Leafmould strode elegantly across the rug and offered Nelly a napkin to dab her lips with.

'Both our sons suffer from Neinschnoozen Syndrome,' he explained. 'It is a rare genetic disorder that has afflicted just three generations of Leafmoulds.'

'We believe it goes back seven centuries to our original German ancestors,' said Agar. 'Riggll and Rythe are the first Leafmoulds to have Neinschnoozen's in over two hundred years.'

'No fear – no sleep,' said Agar. 'That is how Neinschnoozen Syndrome works.'

Nelly's eyes drifted around the antique furnishings of the room. She could almost taste two hundred years of history floating in the dust of the air.

'But you can't leave Badley Hall,' she protested. 'It's your ancestral home.'

'The children come first,' said Leafmould. 'If

there is nothing that can scare them here, then we have no choice but to seek a more frightening home somewhere else.'

'But where?' said Nelly.

'A cave, perhaps,' said Leafmould. 'We have heard that underground caverns by the sea can be particularly frightening, especially at high tide when the cave begins to fill up.'

'Yes! If the cavern filled up at bedtime, just as it was getting dark, we imagine that could be extremely frightening,' said Agar.

Nelly's jaw fell open. 'You can't live in an underground cave! It's far too dangerous, not to mention damp and smelly. What about all your furniture? What about your rugs? And the suits of armour at the top of the stairs? Everything would turn to rot or rust!'

'We have to put the children first,' whispered Leafmould. 'Children need their sleep.'

'And no children need sleep more than Riggll and Rythe,' whispered Agar.

Nelly sighed heavily. 'But surely there is

something we can do to frighten them?' she said.

'We have tried everything,' said Leafmould, shaking his head with resignation.

'We moved their nursery into the dungeon when they were little, and filled the room with rats.'

'But that didn't work,' said Leafmould. 'We moved their bedroom to the front of the north wing, so that it would overlook the family cemetery.'

'We even opened up a couple of the coffins so that the children could look down into them from their bedroom window before they went to bed,' said Agar.

'But that didn't work either,' sighed Leafmould.

'We've even had an incorcism,' said Leafmould.

'What's an incorcism?' asked Nelly.

'It's the opposite of an exorcism,' said Leafmould, striking up another gentlemanly pose beside a high-backed Queen Anne chair. 'Instead of asking a priest to drive evil spirits *out* of your house, you ask him to drive some *in*.'

'We hired a whole bedroom full of ghosts,' said Agar.

'I didn't know you could hire ghosts,' said Nelly.

'Headless ones, chain rattlers, poltergeists, all sorts. We had so many ghostly cold spots in the room that the bedroom curtains froze solid.'

'But the children weren't frightened at all. They just put ten pairs of pyjamas on to keep warm,' sighed Leafmould.

'So Badley Hall *is* haunted!' gasped Nelly.

'Not any more,' said Leafmould. 'We gave up with the ghosts in the end and sent them back to the rental company. It was costing us a fortune to heat the house.'

Nelly's eyes widened at the very thought of a bedroom full of cold spots and spooks. If that hadn't frightened Riggll and Rythe, what on earth possibly could?

'Have you tried really scary bedtime stories?' she asked. 'I know some brilliantly creepy ones.'

'You're welcome to try,' said Leafmould, picking a piece of stinging nettle leaf off the Persian rug and dropping it into the brass coal scuttle.

'What about scary movies?' said Nelly. 'Have Riggll and Rythe seen *Return of the Brain Suckers* or *Frightmare on Gloop Street*? I've heard they're meant to be dead scary.'

'The children thought they were comedies,' sighed Agar.

'We've tried leaving their windows open at night and telling them that a headless Huffaluk with three axes is going to creep in when the clock strikes thirteen and chop them up into little pieces . . .' Agar continued.

'But they didn't believe us,' said Leafmould. 'We even had a second extra number added to the face of clock tower and told them that when the clock struck fourteen a legion of zombie Dendrilegs would crawl out of the gravel on the driveway and wreak terrible havoc on any Muggot children who were lying in bed with their eyes open.'

'And so they stayed up all night by the window hoping it would happen,' sighed Agar.

'We've tied hangman's nooses to the trees in the orchard, we've let the grass grow into a horror-house tangle of thorns and stingers, we've let the house overrun with spiders, we've even bought an unwelcome mat,' she went on.

'Not to mention coating the front door with expensive wax,' grumbled Leafmould.

'We've even loosened all the floorboards upstairs so that every one of them creaks.'

'But nothing frightens Riggll and Rythe in the slightest.'

Nelly turned to look at the two brothers and shook her head slowly. 'I wonder if you would be so kind as to show me their bedroom?' she murmured. 'Maybe I can think of something that you haven't.'

'Goodness!' said Leafmould, looking at the portico clock ticking softly on the mantelpiece. 'It's almost eight o'clock! Agar and I really should be leaving.'

Agar adjusted her barbed-wire necklace in a mirror on the far wall and then placed a small bowl of nibbles on a table next to the arm of Nelly's chair.

'Please tuck in while we are out, Nelly,' she snuffled.

'I certainly will!' smiled Nelly. 'What are they?' she asked.

They looked like gog toenails.

'They're churly freeps,' laughed Agar. 'I made them myself. It's a family recipe.'

'I'll tell you what, Nelly,' said Leafmould, stroking his cravat, 'why don't you ask Riggll and Rythe to show you around our home?'

'I'll just try one of these first,' said Nelly, 'I bet they're delicious.'

Leafmould and Agar left the drawing room to fetch their blazers from the coat stand.

Nelly dipped her fingers into the bowl, gave a churly freep a sniff and popped it into her mouth.

'OK boys, why don't you show me to your r—'

Nelly suddenly clutched her hands to her throat and began to gasp. Her eyes bulged like pickles and her face began to turn blue.

'I'm poisoned!' she cried, sliding off the leather-studded armchair and dropping to her knees. 'I'm dying, Riggll! I'm fading, Rythe! Please help me!'

Riggll and Rythe walked across the room and stared down at the carpet.

'My stomach's on fire! I'm choking, I'm fading fast, and your parents are out of the room, so if I'm dead when they come back, you might get the blame and you could end up in prison or they might even bring back the death penalty especially for you,' gasped Nelly, 'how do you feel about that?'

'Not frightened,' said Riggll.

'Oh, well,' said Nelly, standing back up and brushing herself down. 'Never mind, it was worth a try. Why don't you show me around the Hall?'

8

'That's the fourteenth bedroom over there,' said Riggll, with an indifferent wave of his pincer.

'That's the tenth bathroom down there,' said Rythe, dismissing another oak-panelled door with a shrug.

Nelly was being given a not-so-grand tour of Badley Hall by two Muggot brothers who had seen it all a million times before.

'Slow down!' said Nelly, grinding to a halt at the top of one of two opposing stone staircases that swept majestically down into the main entrance hall. She wanted to take a closer look at the armoury display.

'Why haven't these suits of armour got any arms?' she asked, running her fingers across a rusting warrior breastplate.

'You don't need armour if you've got these,' said Rythe, holding up both his pincers. 'Muggot pincers are arrow proof, crossbow proof, sword proof and cannon-ball proof.'

'Aahh, but what about boiling-oil proof?' challenged Nelly. 'What if a Muggot army was trying to scale a castle wall and the soldiers inside the castle tipped boiling oil over the battlements?'

Riggll and Rythe looked at each other and allowed Nelly to elaborate.

'Shall I tell you what would happen?' cackled Nelly. 'The Muggot warrior would raise his pincers to protect himself but the burning oil would pour all over him, turning his pincers orange like a lobster thermidor! They'd sizzle and boil and steam and whistle. They might even drop off! How frightening is that?' asked Nelly hopefully.

'Not very,' shrugged Riggll.

'Not at all, actually,' said Rythe. 'He'd just grow some new ones.'

'Can Muggots do that?' asked Nelly, throwing a

distracted glance to the foot of the south staircase.

'Afraid so,' said Rythe.

Nelly sighed inwardly and then turned and waved. Agar and Leafmould were ready to leave for their bridge party.

'Our taxi's here, Nelly,' called Leafmould, looking particularly smart in a blue silk cravat and orange blazer.

'Be good for Nelly, won't you, children?' said Agar, bending her beetle legs slightly for Leafmould to slip a lilac and yellow striped shawl over her shoulders.

'We will,' snuffled Riggll and Rythe.

'You carry on with your tour of the house, Nelly,' called Leafmould. 'We'll see you at twelve midnight. We won't be late, we promise.'

'Glad to hear it,' said Nelly, with a wink. 'I wouldn't want to be here when the clock strikes thirteen,' she shivered, 'because there's going to be a full moon tonight, and everyone knows what happens when the moon is full, don't they? The Hound of Montelimar leaves his kennel at the foot of Bootlace Hill and stalks the grounds of Badley Hall in search of fresh Muggot children to eat!'

'Not scary,' said Riggll.

'There's no such thing as the Hound of Montelimar,' said Rythe.

'Keep trying,' gulloped Leafmould, escorting Agar to the front doors of the Hall and shaking them furiously with his pincers. 'Whose idea was it to dip these damn doors in wax?' he cursed.

'Yours, dear,' sighed Agar, leading him in the direction of the tradesmen's entrance. 'Come on, we'll have to walk the long way round again.'

Nelly, Riggll and Rythe watched from the top of the south staircase as Agar and Leafmould scuttled hurriedly out of the hall.

'BOOO!' screeched Nelly, wheeling round suddenly and thrusting her fingers centimetres from the tips of the brothers' noses.

'Not scary,' smiled Rythe.

'I wasn't trying to be scary,' fibbed Nelly, wiggling her fingers like a crab and then pointing

them up at the ceiling. 'I was simply saying BOOO
. . . tiful chandelier you've got up there.'

'We'll believe you,' smiled Riggll, looking at
his brother with a smirk.

'You can't frighten us, Nelly,' said Rythe,
leading her past the armour display towards yet
another corridor of bedrooms.

'We'll see about that,' smiled Nelly. 'Now tell
me which of these bedrooms is yours?'

Riggll and Rythe did an immediate about turn
and swung their largest pincers in the direction
of the opposite staircase.

'North wing,' they said, beetling past Nelly and
beckoning her to follow.

'This house has got more wings than a KFC
bargain bucket!' gasped Nelly, struggling to keep
up as the brothers forged ahead through a maze
of cobweb-cloaked corridors.

'Bedroom forty-six,' said Riggll, finally halting
outside another oak-panelled door and pushing
it open with his pincer.

Nelly stepped into the room and turned her

head slowly in all directions. It was like a chamber of horrors. Death masks hung from the ceiling on wires and grinned gruesomely at a four-poster bed carved with gargoyles.

The mirror above the mantelpiece was cracked, painted cupboards were peeling and the bedspread was embroidered with vampires.

In each corner of the room black candles cascaded with frozen wax and tapestries of mediaeval torture scenes hung sombrely from three walls. Stuffed rats in glass cases lined the

fireplace and on a chair at the foot of the four-poster bed lay two pairs of skull-and-crossbone-motif pyjamas.

'We share the same bed,' smiled Rythe, shooing a spider the size of a football off his pillow. 'Sharing's much more fun, especially if you can't get to sleep.'

Nelly walked sombrely across the room and peered through the checkered panes of a grimy, mullioned window.

'Father leaves the window wide open at night, so the bats can fly in,' said Riggll.

'But they don't frighten us either,' said Rythe.

Nelly stared downwards at the family cemetery and nodded grimly.

'How old are the graves?' she asked, too high up to read the headstone inscriptions.

'Our great-great-great-great-great-great-grand-muggot died in 1596,' said Riggll.

'He caught the Purple Plague,' said Rythe.

Nelly stared pensively from the window. Impenetrable tangles of weeds and thorns choked the view in every direction. Where once there were orchards, now there were brambles; where once there were fountains, now there was dust.

'Don't you find this house just a little bit scary?' she asked, running her finger through the grime on the window pane.

'Not in the slightest,' said Riggll, with a shrug. 'Shall we move on?'

Nelly turned away from the window with a frown. The evening sunlight was beginning to fade from the garden and there were still more rooms to see. 'Lead on,' she said, with a wave.

Giant spiders appeared to be at home in every room, hanging like boxers' punchbags from glass chandeliers and spinning candy-floss-thick webs across windows, ceilings and doorways.

'How big do gigantulas grow?' Nelly asked, watching in amazement as the thick, bristly legs of a particularly large female dragged something across the landing into bedroom ninety-three.

'About two metres round,' answered Riggll.

'Not including the legs,' added Rythe.

'My dad would die of shock if he saw a spider that big,' Nelly gasped, pressing her nose to the window of bathroom seventy-eight to watch the sun dip slowly out of view. The eerie gloom that had settled over the garden was beginning to creep into the house.

'Let's press on,' she said.

After the ninety-third bedroom, the fourth billiard room and the seventh library, Nelly had begun to feel like a Japanese tourist. Riggll and Rythe had done their duty admirably, leading Nelly through the north, south and east wings of the Hall despite their obvious indifference to all the antiquities on parade. It was time to call it a day.

'OK, here's the deal,' said Nelly, clapping her hands. 'You go and put your pyjamas on and I'll meet you in the main entrance hall in ten minutes.'

'What are we going to do?' said Riggll excitedly.

'Something scarier than you could possibly imagine!' hissed Nelly. 'We're going to pretend it's Hallowe'en!'

'What's Hallowe'en, Nelly?' asked Rythe, rubbing his pincers together like a grasshopper and blinking at her with inquisitive buttermilk eyes.

'Hallowe'en is the night of the dead!' she shivered, swaying left and then right. 'It is a night of fear and dread. Of ghosties and ghoulies, and shadows that come alive in the dark!' she hissed. 'It is a night so terrible and so scary, don't be surprised if you wet yourself!' cackled Nelly, getting a little bit carried away.

'Sounds great fun!' laughed Riggll. 'See you in ten mins!'

9

The clicketty-clack of beetles' feet on stone steps told Nelly that Riggll and Rythe were returning down the north staircase.

'Darkness is falling,' cackled Nelly, peering up at them from the gloom of the main entrance hall. 'We will have just enough time to prepare our Hallowe'en masks!'

Riggll and Rythe skipped down the staircase in their skull-and-crossbone pyjamas and waited excitedly for some instructions.

'OK,' said Nelly, striking a zombie-like pose. 'We need some pumpkins.'

The shadowy outlines of the Muggot brothers stood motionless at the foot of the north staircase.

'What's a pumpkin?' asked Riggll.

'It's a big orange vegetable, about the size of

a football,' explained Nelly. 'They're full of seedy mush that you need to scoop out,' she expanded, 'before we cut scary faces out of the shells!'

There was a snigger and a snort.

'Scary vegetables, Nelly?' laughed Riggll. 'You can't frighten us with vegetables!'

'Don't be so sure!' cackled Nelly. 'Wait till you see what I do with them after the scary faces have been carved!'

'What *do* you do with them?' asked Rythe, a little intrigued.

'Aha!' cackled Nelly. 'That is for me to know and you to find out!'

'How about weep pods?' asked Rythe. 'We've got loads of those in the pantry – Mother uses them for her stews. Will they do?'

'Are they orange?'

'No, they're green,' said Riggll, 'but they are big and round and we can pour all the weeps out of the middle.'

'OK, weep pods will have to do,' said Nelly. 'I'll

need candles too!' she cackled. 'Bring as many candles as you can find.'

As Riggll beetled away into the darkness in search of weep pods and candles, Nelly scanned the floor. 'We'll set up Hallowe'en camp here!' she said, pointing to the middle. 'Rythe, will you help me roll back the rug? I don't want to drip candle wax on it.'

Rythe nodded dutifully and took hold of the hall rug at one end.

'We'll roll it towards the front doors,' said Nelly. 'It'll be out of the way there.'

With a heave and a shove, the fine tapestried rug was Swiss-rolled out of harm's way and a night camp established in the middle of the cold stone floor. Nelly and Rythe sat cross-legged on the flagstones of the entrance hall waiting for Riggll to return.

'Weeps ahoy!' said a familiar voice from the shadows. Riggll was returning from the pantry. 'I've got the seven biggest ones!' he snorted, beetling back and forth and placing the unusual-looking vegetable pods in a pile on the floor.

'Did you find any candles?' asked Nelly.

'Ten,' said Riggll, dropping a clatter of large white candles and a box of matches into their midst, 'but you'll have to light them because we're not allowed.'

'No probs,' cackled Nelly with a rub of her hands. 'Fear for your lives, young Muggots!'

Riggll and Rythe sat cross-legged in the gloom as Nelly lit a candle and heaved a large weep pod through the half light towards her. It had the coarse, green skin of a watermelon and the weight of a large bag of potatoes.

'I need a sharp knife,' said Nelly, leaning forward to plan her first incision.

'We don't use knives,' said Riggll through the gloom.

'I can't cut a scary face out of it without a knife,' sighed Nelly. 'What do you use instead of knives?'

'These,' said Riggll, with a shadowy snip snap of his pincers.

'I can get you a spear,' gulloped Rythe, pointing

up the south wing staircase to the armour display.

'Er, I don't think a spear would be a very appropriate instrument,' said Nelly. 'Have you got anything else?'

'We only have these,' said Riggll, snip snapping again. 'We use our pincers for everything.'

Nelly placed her hands on her knees.

'Then you do the carving and I'll do the teaching,' she said. 'Let's give these weeps the Hallowe'en creeps!'

10

Riggll and Rythe set about slicing the lids off the weep pods.

'I've always wondered where weeps came from,' said Nelly, peering inside a pod at the fresh weeps. 'Some Squurm friends of mine had a frozen packet in their freezer.'

The weeps inside the pods were like chrome-plated Maltesers, light as air but hard as bullets.

'Are you sure you can eat these?' she asked, lifting one out and trying to squeeze it between her finger and thumb.

'They have to be boiled for two days first,' gulloped Riggll, plunging a pincer inside a pod and scooping a pincerful out.

Nelly dropped her weep on to the floor and

watched it roll like a ball bearing into the candlelit darkness. She was thankful that she hadn't tried to crunch one with her teeth.

'I'll get a sack to put them in,' said Riggll, scurrying back to the pantry.

It was a big sack. A weep sack evidently, triple perforated for freshness and double stitched down both seams for extra strength.

Nelly and Rythe took hold of a corner each as Riggll emptied each pod in turn. They clattered into the sack like silver marbles, leaving it bulging at the seams.

'Help me drag the bag out of the way,' Nelly said, 'then we'll get on with the carving.'

'Leave it to me,' smiled Rythe, raising the sack one-handed from the floor with the ease of a forklift truck. 'I'll put it over here for now,' he said, depositing the sack in the shadows near the tradesmen's door.

Nelly lifted the candle from the floor and raised it to the ceiling. With a ceremonial sweep of her arm she lowered her eyes to the floor.

'Beware, Muggot brothers, for Fright Time is upon us!'

Riggll looked at his brother and smiled. 'Not scary,' he whispered.

'Disciples of the dark,' cackled Nelly, 'help us carve the scariest faces imaginable into all seven of these Hallowe'en masks. Then truly we will behold the horror of the night.'

'What does a scary face look like?' asked Riggll, lifting a weep pod into his lap.

'Three eyes!' cackled Nelly.

'That's not scary,' said Rythe.

'Four eyes!' cackled Nelly.

'That's not scary either,' said Riggll.

'Ten eyes then!' said Nelly. 'And sharp, jagged teeth!'

'How many mouths?' said Riggll, setting to with his pincers.

'Two! No, three!' said Nelly, with a ghoulish moan. 'Oh, you decide!'

Riggll and Rythe did their Muggotty best, using their pincers like craft knives to carve an assortment of grotesque eyes, mouths, ear-holes, nostrils and open scars into the seven weep-pod shells at their disposal.

'Tell me when you've finished,' moaned Nelly, lighting three more candles and floating like a phantom through the halo of light. 'And then I will cast the final spell.'

'Finished,' said Riggll, leaning back to admire his handiwork.

'Finished too,' gulloped Rythe with a wave.

Nelly swooped like a night spectre towards the circle of light and passed the palms of her hands across each brother's face in turn.

'Close your eyes, my brethren. Close them tight, while I summon the dark Spirits of the Night! And don't open them till I say so,' she added with another swoop.

Riggll and Rythe closed their eyes and listened curiously as the squeak of Nelly's trainers and a strange, demonic chant began to echo around the room.

'*Masks of Satan*

Pods of weep

Be sooooo scary

That Riggll and Rythe can't help but fall asleep!

'Open your eyes, then ... slumber!' roared Nelly, with the spell-breaking cadence of a wizard.

Riggll and Rythe opened their pale, milky eyes and turned slowly in all directions. Green weep-pod masks with candlelit eyes leered at them from every shadow. There was a fiery-eyed mask on two of the stair posts, another on the fireplace mantelpiece. A six-eyed, three-nosed mask stared menacingly from the doorway leading to the tradesmen's entrance, and a seven-eared, twelve-fanged monstrosity glared at them from the coat stand.

'What do you think?' cackled Nelly, wiping her hands on an imaginary witch's apron.

'Very pretty,' said Riggll.

'Yes, really pretty,' said Rythe.

Nelly's shoulders dropped.

'PRETTY?' she stomped. 'It's not meant to be pretty, it's meant to be scary!'

'Well I think it's very pretty,' said Riggll. 'Especially the one with three ear-holes and jagged nose over on the long seat.'

'Yes, that's my favourite too,' said Rythe.

Nelly sighed and sat down cross-legged on the floor. 'PRETTY?'

It was time for a rethink.

Riggll and Rythe waited patiently in the candlelit darkness of the entrance hall, intrigued to see what Nelly would conjure up for them next.

'Would you like us to turn the lights on?' whispered Rythe, as nine distant chimes from the clock tower drifted through the darkness from the south wing. 'It's getting pretty gloomy in here.'

Nelly raised her hand and wagged her finger like a school teacher. 'No way. Candlelight will be much more scary,' she whispered.

'If you say so,' chuckled Rythe.

Nelly sat silently for a while and then broke dramatically from her pretend trance to leer with gargoyle stares at Riggll and Rythe.

171

'Take me to your dungeon,' she said with a ghoulish cackle. 'For I have stories of deep, dark terror to tell!'

'Not scared,' said Riggll with a smirk and a shrug.

'You haven't heard them yet!' said Nelly indignantly.

'Still not scared,' said Riggll, ambling back to the drawing room to retrieve the bowl of churly freeps.

'You will be scared when you hear them!' insisted Nelly, calling after him into the dark.

'Won't,' munched Riggll, returning with their Hallowe'en nibbles.

'Will!' said Nelly, taking two large candles and motioning to Riggll to lead the way.

Riggll's oustretched pincer glistened in the candlelight as he pointed the way through the darkness to the main north wing corridor. The shadows in the entrance hall began to flicker and dance as Nelly took her first candlelit strides across the hall.

'I bet it's going to be really spooky down there!' cackled Nelly.

'Not at all,' said Rythe, leading Nelly past the staircase and along the wood-panelled darkness of the corridor.

'Well it will be when I get there!' said Nelly, with a demonic cackle.

'If you say so,' sniggered Rythe, crunching down on another churly freep.

Nelly peered blindly into the tomb-like darkness of the corridor, and tried to throw the light from her candles as far forward as she could.

'Are those your ancestors?' she whispered, staring sideways at lines of portraits that were leering at her from both sides of the panelled walls.

'Yes,' said Rythe. 'That's Great Uncle Leedl. He lost an eye in the Battle of Beg Blerg.'

Nelly paused and raised one of her candles to Great Uncle Leedl's nose. A solitary, yellow-varnished eye glared fiercely back at her.

'And this is the dungeon,' said Riggll, sweeping

his pincer through the shadows towards a heavily-timbered door.

Nelly stuck her tongue out at Great Uncle Leedl and hurried on through the darkness to where Riggll and Rythe were waiting.

'Excellent!' she cackled, throwing the light from her candles across the heavy wooden door. Riddled with woodworm, battered with age, it was everything Nelly had imagined a dungeon door would be.

'After me!' she cackled, handing Riggll a candle while she heaved back the huge iron bolt. Rust from the bolt powdered the stone floor like burnt icing sugar, and the black hinges groaned as the dungeon door creaked open.

'Is that fear I can smell?' whispered Nelly mischievously, stooping through the low arch and placing her foot on the first dungeon step.

'No, it's the sewers,' said Riggll. 'They always whiff a bit at this time of year.'

'Even better!' said Nelly, croaking like a wizard's bullfrog. 'Let us descend. Let us descend to this foul-smelling hellhole of fear and torture!'

'Anyone want a churly freep?' asked Riggll indifferently.

'Don't mind if I do,' said Rythe.

Nelly took command of both candles again and held them out in front of her like a zombie.

'I am the walking dead,' she groaned. 'Come walk with me into the bowels of the night. Come slither with me where the night-worms writhe. Come hear my stories in this dungeon of despair, for I am the Devil's Storyteller, sent from the fires of hell itself.'

Nelly held the candle below her chin and turned to Riggll and Rythe with staring, zombie eyes.

'Would you like a churly freep, Nelly?' said Riggll, holding out the bowl.

Nelly ignored him and continued her teetering journey down the dark, spiralling vortex of dungeon steps.

'It's a long way down, isn't it?' wavered Nelly, finding it difficult to stare ahead of her like a zombie *and* see where the next step was at the same time.

Fifty-seven spiralling steps down, Nelly turned

giddily and raised both candles above her head. The milky-grey eyes of her Muggot companions glowed back at her in the darkness.

'Is this the bottom?' she asked hopefully.

'Yes,' said Riggll. 'You can stretch your legs out a bit here.'

With every step that Nelly took into the dungeon darkness something crunched beneath her feet. Nelly lowered the candles towards her knees and examined the floor. She was standing on a carpet of rat bones.

'Many legs have been stretched here,' she cackled, waving the candles like incense burners at the ancient torture equipment that had rusted fast to the glistening dungeon walls. 'I shall tell you the story of one such pair of legs – terrible, fearsome, spiny legs of old they were . . . dragon's legs, in fact.'

'Not scary,' said Riggll.

'*Spiky* dragon's legs, covered in boils and poisonous fleas . . .' elaborated Nelly.

'Not scary,' said Rythe.

177

'Purple Plague-carrying fleas!' cackled Nelly, finding some extra inspiration from the family cemetery. 'With teeth as sharp as needles and a bite as deep as a hellhound's!'

'Still not scary,' sighed Riggll, blinking impassively in the darkness.

'*Haunted* legs . . .' hissed Nelly.

'Still not scary,' said Riggll.

'With voodoo claws.'

'Still not scary,' agreed Rythe.

'Haunted, scary, voodoo claws dipped in snake venom SOOOO poisonous and SOOOO dangerous that one scratch would paralyse you in two seconds flat!'

'Still not scary,' sighed Riggll.

'And then your head would fall off!' added Nelly.

There was a pause.

'And your pincers would turn green and your brain would explode,' said Nelly.

The dungeon fell silent. Nelly lowered her candles and waited hopefully in the darkness for the sound of Muggot snores.

Instead, the eerie silence was shattered by the soft crunch of churly freeps.

'OK, you win,' said Nelly with a sigh. 'Let's go back upstairs.'

It took a lot more effort to climb the dungeon stairs than it did to descend them. The calf muscles in the back of Nelly's legs were tighter than banjo strings by the time she emerged, panting, through the low, stone-arched door at the top.

She placed the candles carefully down on the flagstone floor and took some deep gulps of fresh air.

Riggll and Rythe peered at her through the half light and placed their glistening pincers reassuringly on her shoulders.

'That's one advantage of living in a big house,' said Rythe, 'you get plenty of exercise every day.'

'Even more when the front doors are stuck fast,' gurgled Riggll.

Nelly puffed hard. The last time she had done any real exercise, she had been chasing next door's cat around the garden.

'I need a drink,' she sighed. 'Dungeons are thirsty work.'

'Lights on or lights off?' smiled Riggll.

'Lights off,' insisted Nelly. She wasn't beaten yet.

11

'Your mum and dad were right, weren't they?' said Nelly, lowering a goblet of demonade from her lips and resting her arm on the studded leather of an antique, high-backed chair. 'About this Nosnoozing Disease.'

'Neinschnoozen Syndrome,' corrected Riggll from the gloom of the drawing room.

'This "No fear – no sleep" problem really is going to take some solving,' continued Nelly.

The shadowy shapes of Riggll and Rythe leaned forward in their chairs as two large, eight-legged silhouettes scurried up their legs and joined them on their laps.

'Have you got names for them?' asked Nelly, squinting across the half light of the moonlit drawing room.

'No, we only adopted them yesterday,' said Rythe. 'They have to leave the bell tower when they're this age or they get eaten.'

Nelly gripped the stem of her goblet. 'You mean she eats her own babies?' she gasped.

'Queen gigantulas eat anything,' said Riggll.

'Not *anything* anything?' asked Nelly.

'Anything with meat in it,' said Rythe.

'But *I've* got meat in,' gulped Nelly.

'Don't worry,' said Riggll, who could see the way Nelly's cogs were turning. 'We're perfectly safe. The Queen never leaves the clock tower.'

'But how does she eat?' said Nelly.

'The harvest spiders take food to her. They leave it at the foot of the bell-tower steps. You saw a harvest spider earlier, in bedroom ninety-three.'

Nelly's eyes drifted into the darkness.

'What time does she eat?' asked Nelly.

'On the stroke of eleven, usually,' said Rythe, 'unless she's still full from Wednesday.'

'What do you mean?' asked Nelly, intrigued.

'Well an estate agent went to the bell tower

to measure up on Wednesday,' explained Riggll.

'And?' said Nelly.

'The only thing that made it back down the steps was his tape measure,' said Rythe.

Nelly placed her hand over her mouth and gasped.

'Only kidding,' chuckled Rythe.

Nelly sighed, leaned back in her chair and stared past the drawing-room curtains at the moon.

Only kidding, eh? she thought. Two can play at that.

With a mischievous smile she raised the demonade to her lips and drained the goblet.

'Have you got any meat in the pantry?' asked Nelly, trying not to smirk. 'A string of sausages would be useful.'

'We don't eat meat,' said Riggll.

Nelly leaned forward in her chair and stared demonically across the shadow-cloaked room.

'Then WE shall be the meat,' she whispered,

waiting to see fear flash across the brothers' eyes.

Riggll and Rythe blinked at each other. This Nelly the Monster Sitter character was certainly turning out to be top-drawer entertainment.

'We shall be the meat and we shall lie very still at the foot of the bell-tower steps, and wait for the Queen to come down for her dinner,' whispered Nelly. 'And then just as she's about to tuck in to us, we will jump up, blow huge raspberries at her and run away! If we hold our nerve to the very last minute, we'll be able to feel her hot breath on our cheeks. We might even be able to see inside her mouth! If that's not scary I don't know what is,' she finished. 'What do you think, shall we give it a go?'

'Brilliant idea!' gulloped Riggll.

'Top plan, Nelly,' clapped Rythe.

Nelly almost slid off her seat. 'I was only kidding!' she spluttered. 'You don't seriously want to take a trip to the bell tower?'

'I do!' gulloped Riggll.

'Me too!' gulloped Rythe. 'Especially in the dark!'

'Well I don't!' blustered Nelly.

'Nelly's scared!' giggled Riggll.

'No I am not!' protested Nelly.

'Yes you are,' chuckled Rythe. 'You are pooping your pants at the thought of meeting a queen gigantula spider!'

'And maybe getting eaten!' giggled Riggll.

'It will be really dark in the bell-tower tunnel,' cackled Rythe.

'And the ceiling will be thick with scary cobwebs!' teased Riggll.

'And the floor of the tunnel will be teeming with harvest spiders!' cackled Rythe. 'You REALLY DON'T want to go to the bell tower at feeding time, Nelly.'

'Especially on pretend Hallowe'en night!' cackled Riggll.

Nelly stood up and folded her arms defiantly. She was blowed if she was going to be psyched out by a couple of eight-year-olds.

'All right then, let's do it!' she said, calling the brothers' bluff. 'Let's go to the bell tower right now!'

'Hooray!' cheered Riggll.

'Bagsy I hit her in the fangs first!' chuckled Rythe.

Nelly's heart sank like a soufflé. They weren't bluffing at all.

'Don't worry, Nelly,' gulloped Rythe, dancing out of the shadows and hooking his pincer through her arm. 'I'll make sure we don't get eaten!'

'How?' groaned Nelly.

'We'll be tinned meat!' he said. 'Follow me!'

12

'Are you sure it will be OK if we borrow them?' said Nelly, tapping her breast plate with a clang. 'I really don't think your parents would be happy if they knew we were putting on the family armour.'

'They're not here to know, are they!' laughed Riggll, passing his head through the hole of a chain-mail vest.

Nelly placed her helmet on to her head and peered through the letter-boxed eye slits. It was darker than ever inside the helmet. 'Look – we really don't have to do this, if you're too scared.'

'I'm not scared!' giggled Riggll.

'Me neither,' chuckled Rythe.

'Then you must tell me the moment you *do* get scared!' said Nelly, twisting her helmet nervously

to the left and pointing herself towards the stairs.

'And if *you* get frightened, Nelly, you *will* tell us, won't you?' giggled Riggll, offering Nelly a spear.

Nelly declined, and instead placed both hands firmly around her candle.

With their armour secured and their helmets in place, the three warriors stepped boldly down the steps of the south staircase.

'How do we get to the bell tower?' echoed Nelly,

suspending leadership duties for a moment to find her bearings at the foot of the stairs.

'Follow the spiders,' said Riggll, pointing his pincer across the hall.

Nelly raised her candle then dropped her eyes to flagstone level. A black, hairy, wagon train of harvest spiders was making scurrying progress away from the entrance hall into the pitch darkness of the far north corridor.

'What are they carrying?' whispered Nelly. 'It looks like groceries!'

'It is,' answered Riggll.

Nelly raised her candle again and stared.

'That one's got a leg of lamb still in a packet!' she whispered, throwing candlelight a little further down the corridor. 'And look at that one!' she gasped, jumping as a spider the size of a guinea pig scurried past her jeans. 'What's that one carrying?'

'It looks like pork chops,' said Rythe, squinting through the visor of his helmet. 'I can't read the label in this light.'

The eerie chimes of the distant clock tower drifted through the darkness.

'It's ten-thirty,' said Rythe, beckoning Nelly into the darkness with a wave of his pincer. 'We need to hurry, Nelly, or we'll miss the fun!'

'But where does all the meat come from?' she whispered, as two packets of kebabs and an oven-ready chicken scurried into the darkness ahead of her. 'I thought you said Muggots don't eat meat?'

'We don't. The spiders ambush the supermarket lorries at night as they drive past the gates,' said Riggll.

'That's where they run their threads,' explained Riggll. 'Right across the road at wheel level, like invisible tripwires.'

Nelly's mind returned to the accident outside the Badley Hall gates. So that was why the Freshco's lorry had crashed. Her breath began to steam the inside of her helmet and her eyes began to blink hard. She couldn't help thinking that she might be about to bite off more than she could chew.

'Is anybody scared yet?' she asked hopefully.

'Of course not!' gulloped Riggll. 'Why? Are you?'

Nelly shook her helmet. 'Of course not,' she winced.

The flickering green light of the Hallowe'en pods was far behind them now and only the raven blackness of the north-wing corridor loomed. Nelly groaned inwardly and hurried further into the unknown.

A little way past the dungeon entrance, her sense of uneasiness began to build.

'Are you sure she never comes out of the bell tower?' she whispered, trying to sound more inquisitive than scared.

'Positive,' said Riggll. 'She's far too big to squeeze down the tunnel.'

Nelly breathed out hard. She wasn't sure whether that made her feel better or worse.

A single phantom chime from the distant clock tower signalled quarter to the hour.

'We'll be turning left soon,' said Riggll, waving his pincer across Nelly's visor.

Nelly peered ahead and raised her candle. Riggll was right. A long trail of sausages was doglegging out of sight about fifteen metres further down the corridor.

'I can see where you mean,' whispered Nelly, swivelling her breast plate to stop it digging into her shoulders. 'Did anyone bring the barbecue sauce?' she laughed weakly, trying to make light of the moment.

'You are funny, Nelly!' giggled Riggll. 'I wish you could come to monster sit us every night.'

Nelly accepted the compliment with a hollow cough and stumbled further on into the darkness.

'Is anyone scared yet? Because if you are, don't be afraid to tell me,' she whispered.

'She really is funny, isn't she, Rythe?' gulloped Riggll.

'She's the best!' snuffled Rythe.

Ten tentative steps further along the corridor, Riggll's pincer lowered from the gloom like a car-park barrier and stopped Nelly dead in her tracks.

'We're here,' whispered Rythe. 'This is where

we leave the main corridor and turn into the entrance of the bell-tower tunnel.'

Nelly gripped her candle with both hands and shuddered as the terrible black eye of the bell-tower tunnel glared back at her, daring her to enter.

Spiders' webs dripped like stalactites from the tunnel entrance and the busy busy scribble scrabble of harvest spiders' legs echoed creepily from deep within the tunnel bowels. There was no end to the tunnel in sight, only a never-ending funnel of grey web, spiralling like ashen candyfloss into the darkness. Riggll and Rythe adjusted their armour.

'I think we've come far enough,' Nelly whispered.

'Nelly's getting scared!' giggled Riggll.

'I know she is!' chuckled Rythe.

'I am not!' fibbed Nelly, lowering the candle to her feet to throw light on another trail of harvest spiders that were doubling back, empty-handed, from the sinister darkness. 'If they can make it back so can we!' she said, stepping boldly into the eerie hellhole and then kicking out at the tangle of tripwires.

Riggll and Rythe scurried in front of her and began scything a knee-deep pathway through the web with their pincers.

'Can you and Riggll see in the dark?' whispered Nelly, kicking a thick drape of web from her trainer. 'Is that why you never ask to use the candles?'

'Pretty much,' said Rythe. 'Riggll and I have spent so many years awake that we just became used to the blackness.'

'How about your mum and dad?' asked Nelly, crunching something underfoot but not daring to look down to see what it was.

'Not really,' said Rythe. 'They sleep too much!'

'Ugh! A rat!' gasped Riggll, suddenly lunging forward with his pincer and thrusting something under Nelly's nose.

Nelly recoiled as she tried to identify the object bobbing in front of her visor.

'Only kidding!' giggled Riggll, as Nelly's candle revealed a polystyrene tray.

'Not scary,' panted Nelly, waving the tray away.

Everywhere her candlelight ghosted, empty meat trays lay scattered and discarded. Packets hung from threads of web, and sheets of polythene wrapping glistened like a sugar frosting.

'She doesn't eat the wrappers then?' whispered Nelly, sliding a blue plastic beef-joint tray to one side with her foot.

'Only estate agents' suits,' joked Riggll.

'I can see the door!' said Rythe excitedly, beetling ahead into the gloom. 'Look down there, you can see where the spiders are leaving the food!'

Nelly shuffled forward with slow, wavering steps and squinted into the darkness. At the end of the tunnel a huge pile of prime butcher's cuts had been arranged by the spiders into a sacrificial offering. A shiver of fear crept down Nelly's spine. Behind the pile of meat, the door to the bell tower glowered, low, squat and menacing. It was studded like a bank vault and secured with huge, rust-pitted hinges.

'Where can we hide?' giggled Riggll, beetling playfully up to the door and lifting up an oven-ready turkey with his pincer.

Nelly began to feel distinctly uneasy. This adventure had gone far enough. Far too far, in fact, and it was time they were heading back. She turned anxiously and squinted blindly back up the tunnel but the tunnel exit was draped in a cloak of gloom.

Rythe's voice echoed playfully from the shadows.

'I've got an idea!' he chuckled, reaching up with his pincers and pulling blankets of spiders' web down from the walls.

Nelly watched in bewilderment as Rythe's flickering silhouette began cutting into the dense quilts of web that hung from the tunnel ceiling and walls.

'What are you doing?' Nelly whispered

anxiously, as Rythe's pincers snipped like dressmakers' scissors.

'One each,' chuckled Rythe, throwing a cloak of invisibility over Nelly's head and drawing it around her body like a shroud.

'We'll wrap the webs around us like a cocoon until she comes down the bell-tower steps – and when she opens the door we'll spring our surprise!'

'You're really not frightened in the slightest, are you?' groaned Nelly, her heartbeat reverberating inside her breast plate.

'Nope!' said Rythe. 'Why, are you?'

'Of course not,' grimaced Nelly, steadying herself with her hand on the tunnel wall.

'OK, this is what we'll do,' giggled Riggll. 'On the stroke of eleven, we'll cover ourselves with our cloaks and stand stiller than statues. Gigantulas are very sensitive to movement and we don't want Queenie to know we're here until the right moment.'

'Stop trembling, Nelly,' chuckled Rythe.

'I'm not trembling,' fibbed Nelly. 'It's just a bit chilly down here.'

'We'll believe you,' giggled Riggll.

'What next?' whispered Rythe excitedly.

'I know what next,' said Nelly, trying to regain control of proceedings. 'Next, the moment we hear her coming down the steps and you begin to feel frightened, we run.'

'But we won't be frightened,' whispered Rythe.

Nelly gulped. 'Er . . . then we wait for the door to open, *then* we run.'

'No, we mustn't run then! Let's wait for her to come right out of the door and right up close to us!' said Riggll.

'Let's lasso her with a rope of sausages!' giggled Rythe.

'I know!' said Riggll, throwing his cloak to the floor. 'Let's hide under the pile of meat and wait for her jaws to close in on us. Just as she's about to crunch down we could all jump up and bash her on the head with a leg of lamb!'

'Brilliant idea!' chuckled Rythe, his eyes twinkling in the candlelight.

Nelly began to feel hotter than a dragon's hanky. What had started off as an adventure had gone further than she could possibly have imagined. Although she had always had a rather unusual liking for spiders, her fondness didn't extend to being eaten by one.

'I really think we should go back,' whispered Nelly.

'Nelly IS getting scared!' giggled Riggll.

'No I am not!' lied Nelly, opening up her cloak to frown at both of the sniggering brothers. 'All right yes I am—'

'LISTEN!' hissed Riggll. 'She's coming!'

Nelly's eyes dropped to the dark, littered floor. The last remaining spiders in the tunnel were evacuating fast.

'She's coming down the bell-tower steps,' giggled Rythe, snatching up a leg of lamb from the pile of supermarket meat and concealing it beneath his spider-web cloak.

Nelly's grip tightened on the candle and her nerves began to fray.

'Run, Riggll! Run, Rythe!' she gasped, throwing her cloak to the floor. With a blind stumble she fled five steps down the tunnel and turned.

'Look, Nelly! I'm pretending to be a T-bone steak!' laughed Riggll.

Nelly stared in horror towards the bell-tower door. Riggll was holding his pincers out in a T-shape and standing beside the meat pile with a broad smile on his pale face.

The ground beneath Nelly's trainers began to shake and the hinges on the bell-tower door began to loosen.

'No, Riggll! No, Rythe! You must run!' hollered Nelly, torn by her desire to flee and her duty to protect the children. 'This isn't fun any more, it's dangerous!'

But Riggll and Rythe were having none of it. They'd never had so much fun in their lives. Rythe had added a tray of kebabs to his weaponry and was preparing to poke the gigantula with the skewers the moment she emerged through the door.

Nelly's face began to dart left and right inside her helmet. Even the shadows in the tunnel had begun to retreat as the gigantula drew nearer.

'Run!' she begged. 'Run!' she pleaded, slamming her candle back down on to the floor and charging back into the darkness to retrieve the two brothers.

Thunderous, booming echoes began to resonate through the tunnel as the gigantula stomped like a nine-legged Sumo down the lower steps of the bell-tower staircase.

'Here she comes!' giggled Rythe, drawing the leg of lamb from out of his cloak and raising it above his head.

'Noooooo!' cried Nelly. 'We really must ru—'

The bell-tower door flew open with a force so great that the flame on Nelly's candle was nearly shaken from its wick. Nelly screamed a silent scream and her eyes turned to saucers as the first gargantuan leg of the gigantula Queen craned around the door and lunged fearsomely into view. It was the length of three broom handles and had more hairs on it than an unswept barber's floor.

Nelly grabbed Riggll and Rythe by the pincers and tried to tug them away from the door. 'For goodness' sake, run!' she cried. 'Run while there's still time!'

The pile of meat trays began to slide as the bell-tower door groaned open and a second and third leg speared into view.

The humungous black body of the gigantula was contorting and squeezing its way grotesquely through the doorway, like a Spacehopper trying to squeeze through a keyhole.

'She's enormous!' squeaked Nelly, yanking at the shoulders of the brothers' breast plates to try and prise them away.

'We told you she was!' giggled Riggll, preparing to bonk the hairy horror on the head with a tray of loin chops the moment it squeezed into view.

Nelly screamed as a glistening pair of giant spider mandibles thrust forward and suddenly punctured the gloom.

'Wait for its nose!' laughed Riggll. 'I want to bonk it on the nose!'

'I'll bonk YOU on the nose if you don't skedaddle!' screeched Nelly, yanking the tray of chops out of Riggll's pincer and pulling him with both arms down the tunnel. 'AND YOU!' she glared, sending daggers through the darkness at Rythe.

Rythe peeped through his cloak. With a reluctant sigh, he dropped his weapons to the floor and shuffled disconsolately away from the meat pile.

'Spoilsport,' he grumbled.

'DON'T WALK! RUUUUUUUUUUUUUUUU UUUUUUUNNN!' bayed Nelly, staring horror-struck at the door.

Five gigantic legs were pressed like car jacks against the frame of the bell-tower door. They were trying to heave the rest of the black-velvet body through. The faintest glimmer of hope flitted through Nelly's mind that the spider would be too big to squeeze through the door. But her hopes were all too quickly extinguished. With a grinding rasp and a blood-curdling roar the entire body of the queen gigantula suddenly ballooned into view. Its bristles crackled like a yard brush against the stone arch of the door and its mandibles flashed like sword blades.

'She's seen us!' giggled Riggll, standing his ground despite Nelly's best attempts to drag him to safety. 'Hey, Fuzzy-face! We're over here!'

Nelly almost fainted with disbelief. Did these two Muggots know no fear at all? She stood, giddy with panic, as the gigantula rose from the floor of the tunnel and sprang to form a protective canopy over the meat pile with her legs.

'Watch this!' chuckled Rythe, darting forward beneath the gigantula's drooling jaws to retrieve a string of chipolatas.

'Back!' he laughed, drawing the chipolatas behind him like a lion tamer's whip and then unleashing them forward with a stinging smack between the Queen's eyes.

There was no whip crack, more a dull, sausagy thud. But the effect was much the same. The gigantula's eyes blazed like hot coals and her jaws bared like a werewolf's.

'*Now* we run!' laughed Rythe, turning with a fit of giggles and racing towards Nelly and his brother.

'RUN, NELLY, RUN!' giggled Riggll. 'She wants to eat us!'

Nelly grabbed her candle from the floor and gulped large helpings of black tunnel air. Despite all her best efforts to put an end to these proceedings an angry queen gigantula was heading their way, and she seemed hellbent on having them as a starter.

Head down, heart thumping, Nelly turned and fled into the darkness.

The flame on her candle bent like a hairpin as she hurtled blindly back in the direction of the north corridor.

'She's getting closer!' laughed Riggll, peering excitedly over his shoulder.

'It'll be funny if we all get eaten!' chortled Rythe.

Nelly couldn't see the funny side of being eaten at all – in fact, the thick shrouds of cobweb dangling from the ceiling of the tunnel made it difficult to see anything. She wiped a fistful of web from her helmet and turned anxiously to peer over her shoulder. To her total dismay, they were only halfway down the tunnel and the gigantula was still following!

'I thought you said she never leaves the bell tower!' cried Nelly, wrenching off her helmet and hurling it to the floor.

'Maybe she's following the light!' giggled Rythe. 'Throw away the candle!'

'But I won't be able to see without the candle,' gasped Nelly.

'You won't see anything if she eats you,' laughed Riggll.

'We can guide you, Nelly,' chuckled Rythe. 'We can see fine in the dark!'

Nelly flapped her free arm in front of her face, trying to clear the cobwebs from her path. But the more she flapped, the more cobweb she gathered.

'Allow me!' said Riggll, moving ahead with pincers brandished.

The weight of Nelly's breast plate was beginning to slow her down but she didn't dare stop to remove it. Feet pounding, heart pounding, head pounding, she sprinted like a turbo mole through the darkness.

'Run faster, Nelly! Run faster!' giggled Rythe. 'She's catching us up!'

The hairs on the back of Nelly's neck began to prickle as the gigantula's breath drew closer. If she didn't act fast, she'd be spider meat for sure.

In a last gasp effort to escape the spider's clutches, she decided to jettison her candle.

In a blind, breathless panic, she lobbed it over her shoulder, thrust out her chest and spurted for home.

BANG! Went her breast plate.

'LOOK OUT' cried Riggl and Rythe.

THUD went Nelly, blacking out in an instant and crumpling unconscious to the floor.

As Nelly dropped like a dead weight on to the flagstones, the tunnel behind her ignited like a firework. The smell of singed spider belched from the darkness and a piercing gigantula roar shook Badley Hall to its very foundations.

Flesh-fried and shell-shocked, the giant spider reared up in the darkness and then rocked unsteadily on three smoking legs. Its eyes were sizzling like scorched currants and its mandibles were charred like burnt croissants.

Riggll and Rythe watched open-mouthed as the smouldering body of the queen gigantula, teetered one way, tottered another, and then wheeled round and scuttled away in the direction of the bell tower.

The two muggot brothers looked at each other and then joined Nelly on the floor in a heap of hysterics.

'How funny was that?!' they chortled, waving their pincers and legs in the air like over-turned beetles.

Nelly's eyelids fluttered like moths' wings as she slowly began to come round. Her head was spinning in the darkness and her chest felt as if a rhino had stamped on it.

'What happened?' she moaned, her mind in free-fall. 'What hit me?'

'A wall did!' laughed Rythe uncontrollably.

'You ran headlong into this wall!' he spluttered, tapping the wooden panels of the north corridor with his pincer.

'But before you did that, you set fire to the cobwebs in the tunnel with your candle,' tittered Riggll, 'when you threw it over your shoulder!'

'You should have seen the look on Queenie's face!' giggled Rythe.

Nelly groaned and her senses reeled. 'What's that smell?' she sniffed.

'Flame-grilled gigantula!' said Rythe, doubling over again in a fit of hysterics.

Nelly groggily placed her palms on the cold stone floor and heaved herself up.

'Has she gone?' she said in a daze.

'Oh yes!' laughed Riggll. 'And she won't be back!'

Nelly leaned against the wooden panelling of the north corridor and waited for her eyes to grow accustomed to the dark.

'I've never been so scared in my life!' she

groaned, rubbing the armour on her chest.

'Really?' chuckled Rythe.

'It wasn't scary, Nelly, it was fun!' chortled Riggll with an echoey clicketty-clack of his heels.

Nelly squinted into the darkness. She could just about make out the silhouettes of two Muggots doing a victory dance across the flagstones.

'I give up,' she sighed. 'There's more chance of me landing on the sun in a rocket made of butter than there is of me frightening you two to sleep. Would you kindly steer me to your bedroom.'

'Lights on or lights off?' asked Riggll.

'Lights on,' sighed Nelly.

13

Nelly blinked hard as electric light was suddenly restored to the corridor. The long, panelled walls leading back to main entrance hall glistened with varnish and the eyes of the ancestral portraits glared down at her with 'told you so' looks.

With a groan and a whimper she staggered to her feet.

'How did Queenie seem when she went back to the bell tower?' asked Nelly, throwing a cautious glance behind her. The tunnel leading down to the bell tower was smoking like a gun barrel and the smell of singed spider hair was still lingering in the air.

'Not happy!' laughed Riggll. 'Would you be?'

'I guess not!' smiled Nelly, padding groggily after the two brothers.

When they reached the main entrance hall, they found the low, phantom-green light still flickering eerily from the Hallowe'en pods. Rythe scuttled forwards to blow them out, but Nelly stopped him before his pincer could lift a lid.

'Let the candles burn themselves out,' she smiled. 'After all, they do look so pretty!'

'Quite agree!' laughed Rythe, placing his pincer on the stairpost and beetling up the first flight of steps. 'Last one in bed's a fuzzy-face!' he chuckled, scurrying to the top of the next flight and flicking the light switch to the north landing.

'Hey, that's not fair!' protested Riggll. 'You had a head start!'

Nelly watched with a weary smile as Riggll's legs beetled furiously up the staircase in pursuit of his brother. By the time she reached the top step she was alone.

'Bedroom forty-six, I believe it was,' she murmured to herself, staring down at the long, timbered floorboards that stretched like a carpet runway into the distance.

She paused for a moment to look at her watch
and then peered across the hall at the silhouette
of the armour collection at the top of the opposite
staircase.

The hands on her watch said twenty-five past
eleven, but the double chime of the clock-tower
clock insisted it was five minutes later. Leafmould
and Agar would be home inside thirty minutes
and Nelly was determined to have Riggll and
Rythe settled before they returned. She set off
down the corridor, replaying her earlier guided
tour through her mind.

When she opened the door of bedroom forty-
six she found Riggll and Rythe's armour
discarded on the floor like dirty clothes.

'Typical boys,' she said, picking up the breast
plates and propping them by the door. Riggll and
Rythe were sitting up in bed with the light on,
wondering what excitement Nelly had in store
for them now.

They were to be disappointed.

'Sorry, guys,' said Nelly. 'It may not be

sleeptime but it most definitely is bedtime.'

'But we *are* in bed,' protested Riggll, sensing that Nelly was about to bid them farewell for the evening.

'Aren't you going to try and frighten us to sleep?' asked Rythe.

'I've already tried,' said Nelly, pulling the bedsheets up to the brothers' chests. 'Believe me, I've tried.'

'Well try again,' pleaded Riggll. 'I'm sure that you can frighten us to sleep, aren't you, Rythe?'

Rythe crossed his pincers under the bedsheets and nodded. Nelly's eyes drifted from the brothers' skull-and-crossbone pyjamas to the death masks hanging from the ceiling.

'I'm wasting my time,' said Nelly. 'You've got stuffed rats on your mantelpiece, open graves outside your window, your floorboards creak, you've got creepy curtains, a creepy bedspread, you've already sent umpteen ghosts packing . . . there's nothing I can possibly say or do.'

'Well, try,' pleaded Riggll.

Nelly the Monster Sitter

'Yes, please try, Nelly,' begged Rythe.

Nelly withdrew her eyes from the witch-burning tapestry on the far wall and sighed.

'OK, if you insist,' she said, perching on Riggll's side of the bed.

She collected her thoughts for a moment and then stared intensely into the two brothers' eyes.

'Once upon a time there was a monster with three heads . . .'

'Not scary,' muttered Rythe.

'Ten heads,' said Nelly.

'Not scary,' said Riggll.

'A hundred heads!' said Nelly.

Both the Muggot brothers shook their heads.

'OK,' growled Nelly, determined to give them her best shot. 'Once upon a time there was a monster with a zillion heads and ninety thousand tentacles and poisonous teeth and fire-breathing ears that was so scary and so frightening and so terrible and so bloodthirsty that you only had to breathe within five miles of him and he would

216

sniff you out, pluck you from your bed and skin you alive with his special Muggot-skinning claws and gobble you down with a glass of your own blood. But even worse, even more terrible, even more terrifying – instead of finishing you off properly, he would keep you alive in his digestive juices. So he could regurgitate you when he was hungry and eat you all over again!'

The two Muggot brothers looked sideways at each other with steady blinks and then nodded.

'Not scary,' they smiled.

Nelly's shoulders sagged. 'Not playing any more,' she grumbled. 'I'm pooped.'

'Oh *pleeeeeeease*!' begged Riggll. 'We were *nearly* frightened, weren't we, Rythe?' he fibbed.

'I was almost shaking,' lied Rythe.

'No you weren't,' smiled Nelly, sliding off the bed. 'I'm going to tidy up and put the armour back where it came from.'

Amidst a barrage of gurgling protests Nelly padded across the creaking floor of the bedroom towards the door. She was just stooping down to pick up the armour when the pocket of her jeans began to vibrate.

'That'll be my dad!' she said, glancing at her watch and plucking her mobile from her pocket. 'He'll be waiting for me outside.'

Riggll and Rythe watched miserably from their bed as Nelly raised the phone, not to her ear but to her nose.

'Ohhh how cute are theyyy!' cooed Nelly, fawning over the screen of her picture-messaging phone. 'It isn't my dad, it's Marina! Her dog has just had its puppies, aren't they CUTIE PIES?'

Nelly ran back towards the bed with her arm outstretched. 'Aren't they beautiful? Aren't they adorable? Look at their cute little noses and their cute little ears! I wonder if Mum and Dad will let me keep one?'

Nelly sat down on the bed to give the two brothers a closer look at Marina's puppies, but Riggll and Rythe were nowhere to be seen.

'Take them away!' came a muffled voice from beneath the bedsheets. 'They're too scary!'

Nelly peered at Marina's picture text and blinked. She looked down at the bedclothes and blinked again. Riggll and Rythe were trembling. They were actually hiding under the bedclothes and trembling!

With a gasp of excitement and a smile as broad as a banana Nelly leaned forward and began to whisper.

'Once upon a time there was a cutesy wutesy little puppy . . .'

'Too scary!' squeaked Riggll, wriggling further down the bed.

'With a little waggy tail and a warm, little wet nose,' continued Nelly.

'Too, too scary, Nelly!' whimpered Rythe, burying his head under a pillow.

'And the cutesy wutesy lickle wickle puppy had an even cutesier wutesier licklier wicklier friend! A fluffy wuffy kitten called Booful . . . who was pink!'

Rythe's pincer wrenched a second pillow from the bed and slammed it on top of his head. 'Stop!' he squeaked. 'Stop!'

'And they lived together in a town called Cutesville with lots of other cutesy wutesy puppies and fluffy wuffy kittens, not to mention bunny wunnies – baby bunny wunnies with cute little pink ribbons tied to their flopsy wopsy ears,' continued Nelly, her voice wobbling from the tremble of the bedclothes.

'Anyway, one sunny wunny day in Cutesville . . .'

She paused. The bedsheets weren't trembling now, they were rising steadily up and down.

Nelly held her breath and slid off the bed. Pinching the bedsheets between her fingers she slowly pulled them back.

Riggll and Rythe were sound asleep and snoring softly. Their milky, tear-drop eyes had slid behind their pale lemon eyelids for the first time in more than eight years and it was all thanks to Marina's picture message!

'I've done it!' she gasped. 'I've really done it! I've actually frightened them to sleep!'

Nelly danced around their bedroom, her heart pumped full of excitement and pride.

'What will Leafmould and Agar say when they get home?' she gasped.

14

'DAMMIT', 'BLAST', 'OOOER', 'LOOK OUT' and 'YOOOOOOOUCH!' were the first words Leafmould and Agar uttered as they entered the candlelit entrance hall through the tradesmen's door, fell over the sack of weeps, skated like lunatics across the floor, tripped over the rug that had been rolled up to make way for the weep carving and crashed headlong into the main doors. The force of the impact sprung the huge, wax-coated entrance doors wide open, sending them tumbling down thirty stone steps and crunching into a heap on the gravel at the front of the house.

Nelly's dad, who was parked outside in his spider-free zone, flicked the headlamps from dipped to full beam and stared in amazement as

Leafmould and Agar got up and dusted themselves down.

With a slight cough of embarrassment, Leafmould straightened his cravat, waved to Nelly's dad, took his wife by the arm and led her back up the steps to the main hall.

Nelly was waiting for them in the entrance, full of apologies but bursting with excitement.

'They're asleep!' she cried. 'Riggll and Rythe are asleep! I know exactly what you have to do!'

Leafmould and Agar beetled up the north wing staircase to see if what Nelly had said was really true.

Nelly's dad watched from the car as the silhouettes of two adult Muggots danced jubilantly across the brightly-lit window of bedroom forty-six. He had no idea what all the excitement was about but he certainly wasn't going to get out of the Maestro to find out.

'I don't like spiders,' he said to himself with a shudder, as Nelly finally returned down the front steps of the Hall and waved a jubilant goodbye to Leafmould and Agar.

She was still flushed with excitement as the car turned away from the house and pootled up the gravel drive towards the main gates.

'They're going to take away the death masks and the witch burning tapestry and the stuffed rats,' she gushed. 'They're going to close the graves in the cemetery and give Riggll and Rythe's bedroom a complete make-over! I've suggested a pink puppy pattern for the wallpaper and some cutesy wutesy bunny fabric for the curtains!'

Nelly's dad frowned and wiped his brow. As hard as he was pushing the pedal, the car was refusing to accelerate. 'The gravel must be slowing us down,' he reasoned.

Nelly flopped back in her seat, flapping the neck of her sweatshirt.

'Is it me or is it getting hot in here?' she asked, reaching up above her head to activate the sunroof.

'It's been a very warm day,' said her dad,

relieved to be within sight of the gates. 'It was all your mum could manage to rustle up a salad for tea.'

Nelly turned to the rear windscreen threw a farewell glance down the driveway at Badley Hall. Leafmould and Agar were still waving from the steps.

'I hope they invite me back!' she said.

'I'm sure they will,' smiled her dad with a sniff.

Nelly yawned for the first time that night and closed her eyes. Scaring Muggots was tiring work.

'Can you smell barbecue?' said Nelly's dad with another inquisitive sniff. 'I'm sure I can smell roast pork, or is it lamb?'

With ice in her veins and needles in her spine, Nelly opened her eyes and craned them slowly upwards to the sunroof.

'STOPPPPPP!' she screamed, banging both hands on to the dashboard of the car.

Nelly's dad slammed both feet on the brakes and closed his eyes in a blind panic as the Maestro skewed to a grinding halt in the gravel. Nelly's seat belt absorbed the force of the forward propulsion and she watched horror-struck as a huge, smouldering shape catapulted from the roof of the car, bounced off the bonnet, crunched into the gravel, staggered through the beams of the headlights and scurried away into the cover of the long grass.

Nelly's dad opened his eyes and darted his head in all directions. 'What's the matter, Nelly? What is it?' he gasped.

Nelly swallowed hard, relaxed her arms and leaned casually back in her seat.

'It's OK,' she said, closing the sunroof. 'I thought I saw a ghost.'

Nelly's dad rested his forehead on the steering wheel and waited for his heart to stop thumping.

'Please don't do that again, Nelly!' he said, turning into the main road. 'I nearly had a heart attack!'

Nelly closed her eyes again and smiled. Her dad would have had a triple heart attack with knobs on if he had seen what she had just seen.

With a shake of his head, Nelly's dad eased his foot down on to the accelerator pedal.

'Well, the good thing is we've got our power back,' he said, surging towards the front gates.

'That's a relief,' Nelly yawned. 'Home, Jeeves!'

15

A whole week went by before a dentist's appointment took Nelly to the top of Bootlace Hill again. As the Maestro motored past the grey-stone perimeter wall, Nelly raised her picture messaging phone from her lap and asked her mum to slow the car down outside the entrance.

Her mum obliged, pulling the Maestro off the road and pointing it towards the main gates.

'That's the kind of puppy you can have,' said Nelly's mum, pointing upwards to the top of the stone pillars. 'They wouldn't cost anything to feed.'

Nelly clapped her hands and laughed. The two-tongued, antlered slug gargoyles at the top of the pillars had been removed and replaced with a pair of cute, polished pink marble puppy dogs, lying on their backs and playing with a ball.

Nelly clapped her hands again and pointed her phone through the bars. The house and grounds were transformed. The lawns were neatly mowed, the fountains on the south and north wing lawns were cascading with crystal-clear water, but, more pleasing to Nelly than anything, the For Sale sign outside the gates had been removed.

'They're staying!' she smiled, triumphantly. 'The Muggots of Badley Hall are staying!'

'Yes, and we must be going,' said her mum, glancing at her watch and swinging the car back on to the road.

Nelly skewed round in her seat as the Maestro pulled away and took a parting photo of the marble puppy dogs through the rear window.

'I couldn't see any wax on the doors, or cobwebs in the windows, and there was even a bell in the bell tower,' said Nelly triumphantly.

'Well, what else would you expect to find in a bell tower if it isn't a bell?' laughed her mum.

'Don't ask,' smiled Nelly, despatching the

picture of the pink marble puppies to Marina. 'You really don't want to know!'

1

The Montelimar Estate was melting under the onslaught of an early-summer heat wave. The putty in the windows had gone soft, the tar on the roads was bubbling, the grass and even the greenfly were turning brown.

But forget ice lollies, forget orange juice, forget cola – it was champagne time in the back garden of 119 Sweet Street. For after only six years of trying, Nelly's mum and dad had got four numbers up on the lottery.

'Can you help me get this out?' winced Dad, bending over double in an attempt to remove the cork.

Nelly's mum leaned forward in her bikini and received the bottle with the steely composure of a hitman. With barely a blink she closed her fingers around the cork and began throttling it into submission.

'I thought we'd get a lot more than a lousy one hundred and forty-seven pounds,' grumbled Asti, wiping a particularly tickly insect from her neck.

'Especially for four numbers,' agreed Nelly, blowing a ladybird from the end of her finger.

'Apparently, we've done quite well for four numbers,' said her dad. 'A friend of mine only got fifty-six quid!'

'Keep your voice down,' whispered Nelly's mum, jerking her head in small, cautious nods towards their neighbour's fence. 'Mrs Lavender might hear you.'

Nelly and Asti turned to the fence and then looked at each other, none the wiser.

'Mrs Lavender got five numbers and the super ball on New Year's Day,' explained Mum in a barely audible whisper, before easing the cork free with a *thwuck* as loud as a rifle shot.

Nelly's dad jumped, Asti and Nelly ducked and Snowball twitched as the cork rocketed towards the patio, ricocheted off the rabbit cage and flew like a scud missile over the fence into Mrs Lavender's garden.

Nelly and Asti watched, nonplussed, as their mum and dad suddenly leaped from their sun loungers, scarpered across the grass and concealed themselves in the kitchen.

'What are they doing?' whispered Nelly out of the corner of her mouth as her mum and dad's faces peeped like naughty schoolchildren from the doorway.

'I don't know,' whispered Asti. 'Maybe they've gone to get some glasses?'

'We've already got glasses,' murmured Nelly, with a nod towards the sun-umbrella table.

The bubbles in the champagne bottle fizzed emerald green in the sunlight as they waited for someone to pour. But both 'someone's were still crouching beside the tumble dryer with their eyes glued to Mrs Lavender's fence.

Nelly and Asti followed their mum and dad's gazes and waited for the next dramatic instalment.

The fence panels shimmered in the fierce midday heat but aside from an empty coconut shell hanging up for the blue tits, there was very little to observe. Nelly's eyes darted back to her mum and dad and then to Mrs Lavender's fence again. Asti's eyes meandered less energetically over to the kitchen door.

Their mum and dad seemed to be wavering, apparently unsure whether the coast was clear or not. Apparently it wasn't, for as they took their first tentative step back into the garden the champagne cork looped back over the fence from Mrs Lavender's side and plopped forlornly on to the grass.

Nelly's mum wheeled round with embarrassment and Dad slapped his hand over his eyes and winced.

Nelly looked at Asti and shrugged her shoulders. It seemed an awfully big deal to be making over a wayward cork. The two sisters sat up on their beach towels and watched as Mum tiptoed towards the fence to pick the cork up off the grass.

Nelly frowned. Her parents owed them an explanation.

As the champagne bubbles surged exuberantly into the glasses, Nelly's mum obliged.

'Mrs Lavender got five numbers and the bonus ball on New Year's Day and was set to scoop over twenty thousand pounds,' she whispered.

'But the next day when she went to claim her prize, she slipped over on some ice outside the newsagent's,' continued her dad.

'And broke her hip,' whispered her mum.

Nelly shuddered. She knew the old lady next door had broken her hip but had no idea how it had happened.

'She doesn't want anyone to know,' said her mum. 'She thinks people will think she's a doddery old fool.'

'Doddery old fool,' muttered Asti under her breath.

Nelly looked puzzled and then pained as her first-ever sip of alcohol fizzed sourly on her tongue. 'But lots of old people fall over on the ice. It happens all the time in the winter,' said Nelly, placing her glass back on the table with a shudder.

'Not when they're holding a winning lottery ticket, it doesn't,' whispered her dad.

Nelly had a hunch that this story was about to get worse.

'It wasn't just an icy day,' winced her mum.

'It was a windy day,' whispered her dad, dropping the level of his voice down to a bat squeak. 'It was blowing a gale.'

'Mrs Lavender let go of her lottery ticket when she fell . . .'

'The ticket blew out of her hand . . .'

'Down the street . . .'

'Up into the air . . .'

'Over the rooftops . . .'

'And out of sight . . .'

'Never to be seen again,' duoed Mum and Dad.

'It was such a shame – she barely gets by on her pension as it is' Mum continued. 'She had all sorts of things planned for that money.'

'She was going to visit her son in Australia,' said Dad.

'She hasn't seen him for thirty-three years,' explained Mum.

'She was going to redecorate her lounge, buy a new sofa and have her garden completely relandscaped. But thanks to that fall her hopes and dreams slipped from her fingers,' sighed Dad.

'We don't want to make her feel worse by celebrating too loudly,' said Mum, cupping her hand over the top of her champagne glass to soften the sound of the bubbles.

Nelly looked at Mrs Lavender's fence and chewed her lip. 'That's terrible,' she whispered. 'Didn't she go into the newsagent's and explain? I'm sure they would have believed her.'

'She was too embarrassed,' said her dad.

'Poor Mrs Lavender,' whispered her mum, placing her champagne carefully on the lawn and then sitting up to adjust the head position of her sun lounger.

As Nelly retreated inside her head to lament Mrs Lavender's misfortune, Asti suddenly exploded into a fit of giggles and snorts. Nelly and her mum and dad stared wide-eyed at her as she wiped her mouth with the back of her hand and then doubled over in a fit of hysterics.

'SSSHHHHHHHHH!' Mum hissed, lurching from the sun lounger and accidentally knocking her champagne glass over on to the grass. 'She'll hear you!' she whispered, glancing anxiously at Mrs Lavender's fence.

But Asti had completely lost it. She dumped her own glass on the table, dropped to her knees and began rolling over and over on the lawn.

'I can't help it!' she gasped. 'I keep picturing Mrs Lavender slipping over on the ice!' she squealed. 'It's so funny!' she squeaked. 'And then the lottery ticket blows out of her hand!' she spluttered.

Nelly and her mum and dad turned white with embarrassment as Asti curled up into a ball in the middle of the sun-bleached lawn and began kicking her legs like an upturned muggot.

'There's something very wrong with that girl,' murmured Nelly's mum, watching her champagne bubbles sink into the lawn. 'I don't know where she gets her wicked streak from. It's certainly not my side of the family.'

'Well it's not my side of the family either!' whispered Nelly's dad.

'I know what side it is. It's the Dark Side,' growled Nelly. 'She was born evil!' At this particular moment, Nelly's mum and dad were inclined to agree.

'I'm going to look for Mrs Lavender's lottery

ticket!' said Nelly, marching back to the house.

Nelly's mum clambered up from the sun lounger and hurried after her. 'Slow down, Nelly,' she puffed, 'it's too hot to be kerfuffling about in this heat.'

Nelly detoured around Asti and then wheeled round on the patio to lecture her mum.

'I'm not kerfuffling, I'm going out there right now to find that ticket for Mrs Lavender. I can't believe that you and Dad haven't been out looking for it for her! Even if I have to lift up every pavement slab and look down every drain hole and climb up on to every roof of every house on the Montelimar Estate, I'm going to see that Mrs Lavender gets to visit her son in Australia and gets a lovely new garden and a new sofa,' whispered Nelly determinedly.

Nelly's mum placed her hands on Nelly's suncreamed shoulders and shook her head. 'Nelly, it's wonderful that you care so much, but it would take us weeks to comb every street on the estate looking for one little ticket.'

'I don't mind how long it takes me,' said Nelly defiantly.

'But she hasn't got long,' whispered her mum. 'If the winning ticket isn't handed in within a hundred and fifty days, then her ticket becomes invalid and the prize can't be claimed.'

As Nelly began calculating the mathematics of the deadline, her dad joined them with the remaining dribble of champagne and two glasses.

'The deadline's today,' he whispered, picking up on the last few words of their conversation. 'One hundred and fifty days from January the first takes us to the thirty-first of May.'

'No it doesn't, it takes us to tomorrow!' said Nelly. 'That gives me two days to look!'

Nelly's dad passed a glass to his wife and began to divide the remaining contents of the bottle equally-ish between the two of them.

'Hey! I haven't had *any* yet!' said Nelly's mum, handing her glass to Clifford and confiscating his slightly fuller glass.

Nelly's dad shook his head and waggled his

glass. 'I'm sorry, Nelly, but it's a leap year this year. There were twenty-nine days in February instead of twenty-eight. That makes the deadline today.'

Nelly's eyes drifted from Asti's beetle impression over to Mrs Lavender's fence.

'Then I've got no time to lose!' she said, turning away from her mum and dad and striding across the patio towards the kitchen.

Nelly stomped past the tumble dryer, with fire in her eyes and steam in her ears. How could her parents even think of celebrating, when poor Mrs Lavender had had such bad luck? And as for Asti, well, if there'd been a hammer and a wooden stake in the cutlery drawer, Nelly would have marched straight back out into the middle of the lawn and put an end to her sister right there and then.

Nelly's mum and dad looked at each other with flustered frowns. Despite the best efforts of an ice bucket, the blistering summer sunshine was already turning their champagne warm and now their daughter was turning up an emotional heat of her own.

Nelly had the bit between her teeth. Nothing was going to stand between her and finding that lottery ticket for Mrs Lavender. Nothing except the very next sentence spoken by her mum.

'Aren't you monster sitting at one o'clock, Nelly?'

Nelly's outstretched foot halted in mid step, somewhere between the ironing board and the cooker.

'THE THERMITTS!' gasped Nelly.

In the brain-boiling heat of the morning, she had completely forgotten that she had a monster-sitting appointment that very afternoon. She couldn't possibly go on a ticket hunt for Mrs Lavender now.

She dropped her hands and sighed. For the first time in her life, monster sitting was the last thing that she wanted to do. She had never met the Thermitts before and would have to travel right over to the far side of the estate to get to their house. Difficult even under normal circumstances, but particularly hard work today.

But Nelly's word was her bond. She was duty bound to monster sit for the Thermitts that afternoon. With a slump of her shoulders, she dropped her very noble thoughts of helping Mrs Lavender and flip flopped glumly into the hallway and up the stairs.

'Pour my champagne on Asti's head!' she shouted down from her bedroom door.

Fighting talk. But it was too late. Her dad had already drunk it.

2

Nelly sat on her bed and gingerly lifted her bikini shoulder straps. Despite liberal dollops of total sun block, she was already turning pink. Pulling a face like a grouper fish, she extended her bottom lip and blew upwards at her forehead. It was sweltering. She had opened all the windows in her bedroom to let in a breeze, but sappingly, there was no breeze to let in.

She stood up wearily and closed her curtains before the sunshine could set fire to her bedspread. As the curtains drew together the daylight gave way to semi-darkness.

Basking in the cool of the shadows for a moment, she laid her hand on the bedside table and tried to muster enough energy to collect her thoughts. She had to forget about Mrs Lavender now and switch to monster mode.

She needed a monster address. See diary. And she needed to check her notes to see if she needed to take anything special with her to the Thermitts'. See diary too.

Seeing her diary, even in a room with curtains drawn, was never going to be a problem. Big, fluffy and strawberry red, it lay like a beacon beside Nelly's monster-sitting phone.

Nelly slid her index finger between the pages like a paper knife, and flipped it open.

It opened at the previous month's Muggot adventure, but with another flip of her finger arrived at today.

Nelly's eyes tripped casually across the entry that she had made on the page almost a week before.

It read: 'THE THERMITTS, 27 BLACKJACK STREET. 1.00 till 4.00.'

She wiped her brow with the back of her hand and stared long and hard at the 'PS'. A frown broke across her forehead as her eyes struggled to comprehend the words that she had written. For in blackberry-purple gel-pen she had double underlined: '<u>SPECIAL REQUEST. DON'T FORGET TO WEAR TWO COATS, THREE SCARVES, TWO VESTS, THREE PAIRS OF LONG SOCKS, TWO PAIRS OF GLOVES AND BOBBLE HAT!!!</u>'

Nelly stood like a loon for a moment and stared at the open page. Even the thought of changing into her sardine sweatshirt was enough to make her sweat. But two coats, three scarves, two vests, three pairs of long socks, two pairs of gloves and a bobble hat? In this heat? No way!

'I'm not going anywhere dressed like that, especially on a day like today!' she mumbled. 'I'll have a quick shower and sling on some shorts and a T-shirt.'

Nelly grabbed the necessaries from her chest of drawers and wardrobe and trotted down the landing to the bathroom. The showerhead spluttered into action, the shower curtain drizzled with cool water and the heat of the day spiralled down the plughole. Nelly closed her eyes and sighed with relief. She'd never known summer temperatures like it. How Snowball managed to cope wearing a fur coat was anyone's guess.

Her thoughts stayed with her pet rabbit for a moment and then switched on to coats of a different kind. Why had the Thermitts asked her to wear two coats of her own, not to mention the bobble hat, scarves and gloves? She didn't know them well enough to know if they were joking but she did know enough about monsters to assume that perhaps they were not.

A nagging doubt began to gnaw at her. If she ignored the Thermitts' request and turned up in shorts and a T-shirt would she offend them? She wouldn't want to do that, in spite of the fierce summer heat. Nelly lifted her face to the showerhead and let the shower sprinkles jacuzzi her eyelids. With a twist of the dial and a shake of her head, she stepped on to the shower mat and reached for her towel.

'I most certainly will *not* be wearing two coats,

three scarves, two vests, three pairs of long socks, two pairs of gloves and a bobble hat to number 27, Blackjack Street!' she determined . . . 'But I'd better take them with me . . . just in case.'

It was a compromise that would mean her stuffing a wardrobe of winter clothes into a summer holdall and lugging it two miles across the estate in blistering heat. But what else could she do?

'I know!' smiled Nelly, padding barefoot back to her bedroom. 'I'll ask Mum for a lift!'

She detoured into her mum and dad's bedroom on the way to wrestle the holdall down from the top of their fitted wardrobes. It was blue canvas with brown leather handles. Its sabretoothed zip could gape wide enough to swallow three caravans. Well, almost. Anyway, it was amply big enough for Nelly's purposes.

Even crammed with all the clothes that the Thermitts had requested her to take, there was still room for some more. Nelly sat on her bed in shorts and a yellow strappy vest and eyed the contents of her wardrobe that still remained.

'In for a penny, in for a pound,' she muttered, extracting her sardine sweatshirt and green jeans.

As she folded them carefully and tucked them beneath the zip of the holdall, she began to get the feeling that today would be a weird one. Call it a hunch, call it 'monster instinct', but as the teeth of the zip closed across the holdall, Nelly was almost certain that 27 Blackjack Street had a bigger than average surprise in store.

3

It certainly wasn't the first time that Nelly had asked her mum for a lift, but it was the first time she had asked her in a heat wave.

'Ask your dad,' said her mum, barely mustering the energy to move her lips. Nelly stared down at the sun lounger. Her mum was flat out, soaking up the rays with the enthusiasm of a flame-grilled burger. Her bikini was flaring fuschia pink in the sunshine and a moustache of perspiration had sprouted across her top lip. Nelly's mum wasn't going anywhere.

Nelly turned to her dad in time to see him shut his eyes tightly and play dead on the sun lounger beside the sun umbrella.

'Dad, can you give me a lift to Blackjack Street?' asked Nelly. 'I've got to be there in twenty minutes

and it's far too hot to walk.'

Nelly's dad closed his eyes a little tighter and then reinforced his unavailability with a none too convincing snore.

'Clifford, we know you're awake,' murmured Nelly's mum. 'Nelly needs a lift.'

Nelly's dad played his ace, keeping his eyes shut tight and sending a thin line of dribble trickling from the corner of his mouth.

'Dad! That's disgusting!' said Nelly, dropping the holdall on to the lawn.

Nelly's mum opened her eyes and then lowered her sunglasses. 'Clifford! Will you stop pretending to be asleep and talk to your daughter? She needs a lift!'

'I need a lift, Dad,' confirmed Nelly.

Nelly's dad lay lifeless for a couple of extra moments and then sat up with a sigh.

'What have you got in there?' he said, squinting into the sunlight at the holdall that Nelly had dropped on the grass.

'Don't ask,' sighed Nelly, stepping into the shade of the sun umbrella. 'Please give me a lift to the Thermitts', Dad – this weighs a ton.'

Nelly's dad groaned inwardly and blew a bead of sweat from the end of his nose. He was partial to a bit of sunbathing himself but had to concede that for his Aztec wife, sun worship was a religion. If anyone had to go, it was him.

'Make her walk,' said Asti, who was stretched out on a beach mat over by the swing. The idea of Nelly crawling on her knees across the Montelimar Estate, dragging a ten-ton holdall and gasping for water, had predictably wicked appeal.

'Nelly can't possibly carry that bag all the way over to Blackjack Street, Clifford,' said her mum. 'She'll die of exhaustion.'

'Definitely make her walk,' sniggered Asti.

Nelly's dad crumpled with resignation and rolled limply off his sun lounger. Why him? Why did *he* have to don the taxi hat again? There he was, quite happily settled on his sun lounger, minding his own business, celebrating his lottery win, when – 'TAXI!' – he had been summoned to perform weekend duties yet again.

'It's a shame we didn't get *six* numbers up on the lottery,' he grumbled, 'we could have bought Nelly a fleet of chauffeur-driven limousines.'

It was only after he had slipped his T-shirt over his swimmers that the Angel of Salvation entered his life.

'I can't take Nelly!' he said suddenly and surprisingly convincingly. 'I've been drinking! I've had far too much champagne to be able to drive anybody anywhere,' he said triumphantly.

Nelly's mum opened one eye. 'You've only had one glass.'

'No I haven't,' said Dad. 'I've had Nelly's glass too, plus that little extra bit that I shared with you. Sorry, Nelly, you know I'd love to run you over to Blackjack Street, but I mustn't drink and drive. It's against the law. I'm afraid Mum will have to take you.'

'I've been drinking too!' said Nelly's mum, sensing that a disastrously unscheduled end to her sunbathing session was rapidly approaching.

'No you haven't,' said Nelly. 'You spilled your first glass on the grass and you only had a mouthful after that.'

Nelly's mum sat up uncomfortably. She needed an escape plan fast. Her eyes darted desperately to the garden table where Asti's unwanted glass of champagne stood warm and lifeless.

'That's mine!' protested Asti, sensing that her mum was about to make a lunge for it.

Nelly's mum bowed her head as a cloud of

resignation passed between her ears.

'All right, Nelly,' she said, blinking ruefully up into the sunshine, 'let me make myself decent.'

As Nelly's mum stood up dejectedly, Nelly's dad flopped backwards triumphantly.

'Sorry, luv,' he said, 'I shouldn't have drunk Nelly's glass of fizz too.'

'No you shouldn't,' growled Nelly's mum, going out of her way to throw a shadow over her husband before walking back to the house.

Nelly followed with the holdall in hand. 'I'll meet you by the car, Mum,' she said, swinging the holdall through into the kitchen and dumping it down on the floor.

'I'll be five minutes,' said her mum.

4

Nelly was standing in the shade of the front porch when her mum appeared, dangling the car keys.

'It's too hot by the car,' said Nelly, frowning at the coral-white glare of the drive.

'It's too hot everywhere,' said her mum, fanning her face with her free hand and walking to the door of the Maestro.

Nelly lifted the holdall from the porch step and lurched her way over to the car.

'Stand back,' said Mum, turning the key in the door and wrenching it open.

Nelly leaped back as a searing plume of heat belched from the interior of the car, singeing the hairs on her knees. The sun had turned the car into a pressure cooker.

Nelly looked down at the molten plastic seat covers. 'I'll melt if I get in there!' she gasped.

Nelly's mum assumed the role of chief firefighter and leaned bravely into the car.

'Find something to put on the seats,' she said, winding down each window in turn. 'We'll be fine once we start driving and the air begins to circulate in the car.'

Nelly unzipped the holdall and pulled out her sardine sweatshirt and jeans. 'I knew you'd come in useful,' she smiled, spreading them like picnic blankets across both front seats.

With the holdall safely stashed away on the back seat and the sunroof fully open, Nelly and her mum pulled off the drive into Sweet Street.

The roads ahead seemed quiet. The usual Saturday traffic had stuck fast to the kerbsides, leaving the route to Blackjack Street relatively clear. As far as the High Street, that is. It wasn't until Nelly and her mum approached the post office that their progress visibly slowed. In fact it did more than slow. It ground to an airless, smog-peppered halt.

'Roadworks,' groaned Nelly's mum. 'What are they digging the road up for now? It's only two weeks since the Gas Board were in.'

Nelly leaned out of her window and peered along a queue of cars that stretched ahead of her as far as the fishmonger's.

'It's a burst water pipe!' she exclaimed. 'There's water all over the pavement.'

'Well wouldn't you just know it!' said her mum. 'Here we are in the middle of a heat wave and the Water Board starts splurging water all over the place.'

'It looks pretty bad,' said Nelly, looking at her watch. 'None of the cars ahead of us are moving.'

'And you know who's going to foot the bill for it all, don't you?' said her mum, who had suddenly become even hotter and more bothered. 'Your dad and I. Oh yes, they always pass the cost of these things on to the customer. We can whistle goodbye to our lottery win, Nelly, because that leaky lot down there are going to need it all to pay for a new pipe!'

Nelly stared at her watch. She was more concerned about being late for the Thermitts than the impact of a burst water main on the local economy.

Nelly's mum slapped the steering wheel impatiently. 'Well you'd better have it while we've still got it, Nelly!' she said, reaching towards Nelly's feet and retrieving her handbag from the floor. 'Dad and I were going to give this to you and Asti this evening, but take it now, before the Water Board nab it. It's your share of our lottery winnings.'

Nelly deserted her watch and then gasped as her mum pressed twenty-five pounds into the palm of her hand and closed her fingers tightly around it.

'Thanks, Mum!' Nelly beamed. 'Thanks A LOT!'

Nelly's mum drummed the steering wheel with her fingers and forced a smile.

'Don't spend it all at once,' she said. 'Knowing our luck it will be another six years before we win again.'

Nelly poked the money into the pocket of her shorts and leaned out of the window again. Three men in orange, sleeveless waistcoats were striding through the flood waters in Wellingtons, trying to shoo a family of ducks from the scene.

'It looks really bad,' said Nelly anxiously. 'I'm going to be late for the Thermitts if we don't move soon.'

Nelly's mum crunched the car into reverse and began inching the Maestro back towards the front bumper of the car that was queuing behind them.

'I'll cut through Freshco's car park,' she said, placing her arm across the back of Nelly's seat and smiling sweetly at the driver behind her.

It was far too hot for road rage and so instead, the driver behind blew some bubble gum cheeks and inched his car backwards too.

'I'm going to be late,' groaned Nelly.

'I'm doing my best,' said her mum, three-point

turning around, bumping the car over a hump in the road, through the brick arched entrance to the supermarket and speeding past a snaking line of shopping trolleys.

'But I'm never late!' said Nelly.

'You can spend that money I've given you on a proper taxi if you like!' said her mum, who was starting to feel a little undervalued. 'If you think you can get there any faster with someone else at the wheel, I'll drop you off right here right now!'

Nelly zipped it. It wasn't her mum's fault that the High Street had sprung a leak, and she certainly wasn't going to waste any of her twenty-five pounds on anything as dull as a taxi fare.

'Sorry, Mum,' said Nelly.

5

After a hot, clammy and sinuous journey through the back streets of the Montelimar Estate, Nelly's mum finally turned the Maestro into Blackjack Street.

Nelly looked at her watch. She was ten minutes late. She slid her sweatshirt out from under her bottom, pulled her jeans from under her mum's and dropped them both into the open zip of the holdall. Her mum slowed the car and began scanning the doors in the direction of number 27.

'It's on the right side of the road, Nelly,' she said. 'It must be a little further down here.'

Nelly flapped the straps of her vest. Despite the open windows of the car, little or no air had managed to circulate. Even worse, the sunshine lasering through the sunroof had cooked her head like a parboiled potato. She touched her centre parting delicately with the tips of her fingers. She wouldn't have been at all surprised to find her hair had bleached blond.

'There's number forty-eight,' said her mum, slowing the car to a crawl and scanning the houses further along.

There was a water sprinkler pirouetting on the front lawn of number 20, but the midday heat had become so intense, the droplets were turning to steam before they could reach the grass. On the driveway of number 22, a sun-loving cat lay dead to the world. Next door at 24 a chamois leather lay like a crispbread on the bonnet of a half-shampooed car. Net curtains hung lifelessly in wide open windows, blackbirds sat motionless under hedges with their beaks wide open and their eyes bulging like glass beads. There was a suffocating stillness about all of the gardens. Oxygen was in short supply the length and breadth of Blackjack Street, and every home appeared to be gasping for breath.

Except, it seemed, for number 27.

As the Maestro drew up outside the driveway of the Thermitts' home Nelly couldn't help noticing that number 27, Blackjack Street seemed to be strangely detached from the heat. There were no colourful hanging baskets wilting in the sunshine on the front walls and no notes to the milkman browning to a crisp on the front step. Every window of the house, both top and bottom, was mysteriously fastened shut. Instead of flaring in the midday sunshine, each individual glass pane looked mattly and flatly blank. In fact, the strange milky-white pallor of the windows gave the house the slightly unnerving appearance of a blind man.

'They don't look very *in*, Nelly,' said her mum. 'Are you sure this is the right address?'

'I'm sure,' said Nelly, reaching over to the back seat to retrieve her holdall. 'Can you pick me up at four?'

'I'll get your dad to do it,' smiled her mum. 'He should have sobered up by then.'

Nelly climbed out of the car and lugged the holdall on to the sun-baked pavement.

'See you at four then. Thanks for the lift,' Nelly called, as her mum turned the Maestro around and melted away in the direction of home.

'Better late than never,' puffed Nelly, squinting up at the sun and then struggling, two-handed, down the Thermitts' path with the holdall. 'I hope I haven't made them late.'

She dumped the holdall down on the black-tiled doorstep and rang a square-shaped chromium doorbell located just to the left of the door. Past experience had taught her to step back after ringing a monster doorbell. Sloppy kisses, prickly handshakes, slithery hugs – there was never any telling how over the top a monster greeting would be.

Nelly took two steps back for luck and waited patiently for the door to be answered. The first tring of the doorbell died away softly, but produced no response from the door hinges at all. Nelly waited a couple of moments longer and then stepped forward and rang the bell again. She stepped back and waited.

'Maybe it *is* the wrong house,' she said, placing her hand on the back of her neck to shield it from the sun.

She fixed her sights on the centre of the door and then leaned forward to inspect the smooth, shiny, white surface. Unlike all the other doors in Blackjack Street, it hadn't been glossed with a paintbrush but was factory enamelled. In fact, unless she was mistaken, the door wasn't made of wood at all. It was made of metal. There was no panelling, no letter box, no Yale lock, no door latch.

It was more like a fridge door than a front door.

Nelly looked down at the holdall of winter clothes and then turned her head slowly towards the bay window just to the left of the front step.

Three small orange eyes were peering at her through a powdery-white pane.

Nelly peered inquisitively as a green, padded fingertip pressed itself to the inside of the window and began to snake across the surface.

'It's writing something!' she gasped. 'It's writing on the window with its finger!' Sure enough, a Thermitt was using the white window pane like a blackboard in reverse. Nelly concentrated hard on each letter as it formed.

'Are

you

Nelly

the

Monster

Sitter?' it read.

Nelly smiled at the three orange eyeholes and nodded. Each of the eyes blinked in turn and then dropped lower down the pane in readiness for the next message.

'Put

your

winter

clothes

on,

please,' it read.

Nelly smiled and then wiped her brow with the exaggerated sweep of a silent-movie star.

'It's too hot!' she mouthed, flapping the straps of her vest and then pointing up at the fireball sun.

The three orange eyes stared impassively back at her through the small eyeholes. Nelly smiled at them and then shifted uncomfortably. She could see nothing more of the Thermitts than their orange eyes. Was it one three-eyed Thermitt or three one-eyed Thermitts? It was impossible to tell through the white-sheeted pane.

What she was sure of was that the back of her neck was burning and if she stood here much longer she was likely to spontaneously combust.

To her relief, the three orange eyes disappeared from the eyeholes in the pane, but to her dismay they didn't appear at the front door.

'Where have they gone now?' she winced, pulling the scrunchee from her ponytail and fanning her long black hair out to shield her shoulders. 'Please open the door,' she gasped.

But the front door remained firmly closed. Nelly groaned. This was far from the monster welcome she was used to. The backs of her legs began to prickle and her arms began to scorch.

'Where are you?' she sighed, taking three steps back and then stepping sideways on to the crispy-fried lawn to survey the bay window from the front.

Nine orange eyes blinked back at her through the opaque, white panes of the front bay. Graffitied into the surface inside the window was another message from the Thermitts. In huge capital letters it read:

'YOU <u>MUST</u> PUT YOUR CLOTHES ON, NELLY!'

Nelly swallowed hard and dry. How could she possibly be expected to dress for winter in a heat wave? She stared back at the window for a moment but the Thermitts seemed unmoved. With a look of puzzled exasperation Nelly walked back to the front step and unzipped her holdall.

With a sweltering struggle she wrestled her sardine sweatshirt over her head. Squeezing her jeans over her shorts and funnelling her toes into a pair of long socks she staggered back to present herself to the bay window.

The nine orange eyes stared impassively back at her. Nelly's body temperature began to soar and the blood in her veins started to boil like chip fat. But the Thermitts seemed unmoved.

'Please let me in!' she whimpered.

The nine orange eyes blinked blankly back at her and then lowered in unison as another green finger pad began to write on the powdery, white surface of the window again.

Nelly was beginning to feel faint. She smiled weakly as the next message unfolded across the pane.

'PUT ALL OF THE CLOTHES ON, PLEASE,' it read.

Nelly swooned. All of them? What – two coats, three scarves, two vests, two pairs of gloves, three pairs of socks and a bobble hat? Surely not. Definitely not in this heat!

She stared at the white panes of the window with pleading eyes but the Thermitts' orange eyes stared unflinchingly back at her. All of the clothes it would have to be.

With a face like a bulldog, Nelly trudged slowly back to the holdall and tugged out her yellow overcoat. Button by button she fastened it up. With a dizzy sigh she plucked out her black puffa jacket. The elasticated trim on the sleeves made it hard to squeeze her arms through, and the thickness of her overcoat stretched the puffa stitching to breaking point. As she inched the zip of the jacket stiffly up towards her chin she turned to the bay window for mercy.

But she was out of luck. The Thermitts had written 'AND THE REST' on the bay window too.

Nelly groaned and reached back inside the holdall. She felt like a double-stuffed, triple-baked, tandooried turkey. But sock by sock, scarf by scarf and glove by glove, she applied the trimmings.

'I'm going to faint,' she gasped as her hands lowered her bobble hat towards her eyebrows.

Her eyelids began to flutter and her knees began to buckle.

'I'm going to die,' she gasped.

Nelly lurched two steps sideways and then one step forward, but before the volcanic rays of the

heat wave could batter her to the ground the door of number 27 flew open.

A billow of icy cold air pillowed into her face, bringing her immediately back to her senses.

Nelly gasped as her cheeks froze and then stared at the wide open door.

Two Thermitts were standing in the doorway cloaked in freezing mist.

'Quick, come inside, Nelly,' beckoned a blubbery, white paw, its single green finger curling invitingly. 'Come inside quickly before the temperature rises.'

Nelly wavered for a moment and then staggered forward like a whale in a bobble hat. As she stepped out of the sunshine and into the house, the arctic chill inside the hallway iced her body from head to toe. The relief was as welcome as it was instantaneous.

'This isn't a house,' gasped Nelly. 'It's a deep freezer!'

6

Nelly dropped her empty holdall and then tugged her scarves down from over her eyes to glean a better look at the Thermitts. But the moment the front door closed behind her, the hallway was immediately plunged into darkness!

Nelly wheeled round blindly, took one step forwards and fell flat on her backside.

'Mind your step,' said a slow drawl.

Nelly's mind reeled in the darkness. It felt colder than a choc ice inside the house, but, even more disconcerting, it was now darker than a polar bear's nose.

'Don't worry, there's daylight in the lounge,' drawled another voice. 'You'll be able to see perfectly in there.'

Seeing wasn't Nelly's main priority right that

moment. Getting back on to her feet was. Not only was she weighed down by enough clothes to fill a jumble-sale stall, the floor beneath her was inexplicably slippery.

'I can't get up!' said Nelly, trying to steady herself in the darkness but finding it impossible to get a grip with her feet.

'Allow us!' said the first voice.

Nelly's legs scrabbled and then kicked as her toes raised off the ground. To her total surprise and slight embarrassment the Thermitts had taken it upon themselves to carry her into the lounge.

'Please come and meet our young son, Nip,' they said.

Nelly's legs dangled helplessly.

'I'll be all right to walk now!' she said. 'You can put me down just here if you like.'

'How about we put you down in here?' said one of the Thermitts.

A door opened and the brilliant white light that ignited in the room, sent a shaft of brightness spearing into the hallway. Nelly blinked hard and fast as her eyes struggled to attune to the light, but before she could muster her senses the door of the lounge closed silently and the room dimmed daylight bright again.

'They *are* fridge doors!' she gasped. 'When you open them the light comes on, when you close them the light goes off!'

'Night or day,' nodded a Thermitt, wrenching the lounge door open from its white rubber seal and then closing it again for a demonstration.

Although an absence of windows had made it unnaturally dark in the hallway there was no need for a light bulb in the lounge. At least not during daylight hours and certainly not on a day as fiercely sunny as today. Even though the bay windows were masked with thick frost, daylight flooded every corner of the room.

Nelly gawped through the narrow gap between her scarves and her bobble hat at every sub-zero feature of the room.

The lounge she was standing in was fashioned like a deep-freeze unit. It had white, ribbed plastic walls that sparkled like fresh snowfall and large bay windows that were curtained with thick frost. Icicles dropped from the ceiling like arctic chandeliers and below, a floor of sheet ice glistened like an ice rink.

'No wonder I fell over!' she gasped, her breath steaming in the cold air.

'Now you know why we asked you to wear all those clothes, too!' smiled the Thermitt closest to her.

Nelly smiled back through her scarves and then reprimanded herself. In the pandemonium of her entry to the house, she had forgotten to introduce herself!

'Nelly the Monster Sitter,' she said, inching her lips up over her scarves and offering up her double-gloved hand for a handshake. 'I'm so sorry I was late . . .'

The Thermitts looked at each other and then smiled with broad, gaping mouths. To Nelly they looked like a cross between walruses and giant three-eyed potatoes. Their skin was mottled pinky-brown and it tumbled in blubbery folds down to their sumo-girth waists. They had jet-black, Eskimo-style hairdos on top of their bodies and ski-length, leathery feet at the bottom. From the corner of their lips blue

barbules hung like catfish whiskers and in the middle of their faces three bulbous orange eyes bulged like satsumas.

'My name is Ig,' drawled the blubberiest of the two Thermitts, 'and this is my wife, Loo.'

Nelly peered over her scarves and directed her arm stiffly towards Ig's solitary, asparagus-green finger. As she closed her gloves around it an icy chill crept through to her palm.

'Pleased to meet you, Ig,' said Nelly, releasing the Thermitt's finger after three vigorous shakes and then extending her arm towards Loo.

Loo shook Nelly's hand politely and then turned.

'Come and say hello to Nip, Nelly,' Loo drawled, skiing on feet the size of French-bread loaves towards the sofa. 'He's been ever so keen to meet you.'

Nelly turned towards the sofa. She couldn't see any sign of a third Thermitt anywhere. The sofa, however, was a sight to behold. It was like a huge sculpted freezer block, cubed in shape and antifreeze blue in colour. Ice cubes the size of bed pillows were scattered like cushions at both ends and a footstool made of lolly sticks was positioned close by.

'He's a bit shy,' drawled Loo, gliding around the back of the sofa and then bobbing down out of view.

Nelly inched her way precariously across the icy floor and then toppled awkwardly on to the glacier-hard seat. There was one advantage to wearing so many clothes. If she did slip over she had the equivalent padding of two mattresses to protect her.

With a series of reverse lurches and wriggles she inched her thickly-padded bottom backwards and pressed herself to the rear of the sofa.

'Meet Nip,' drawled Loo proudly, lowering a mini version of her own feet over Nelly's head and dropping a smaller blubbery potato into her lap.

Nelly leaned back in surprise and then smiled

warmly as the twinkling orange eyes of the junior Thermitt buried themselves into her puffa jacket.

'Hello, Nip,' said Nelly. 'Don't be shy, I've come to have some fun.'

The black, tousled tufts on the top of Nip's head lifted from Nelly's chest and then dived back into the cover of Nelly's puffa padding.

Nelly ran her gloved fingers across the leathery folds of Nip's shoulders and then tickled him somewhere between his waist and ribs.

As the tip of her finger wormed playfully into the folds of his blubber, Nip began to giggle, raising his three orange eyes towards Nelly's spiral of scarves and then smiling at her with his wide, blue-barbuled mouth.

'That's more like it,' said Nelly, easing the little Thermitt forward on to her knees. 'Pleased to meet you, Nip. How old are you then?' she asked.

'He's two, Nelly,' drawled Ig, striking the freezing air twice with the only finger on his hand. 'He doesn't speak yet, but the longer you spend with him, the less shy he'll be, we promise.'

'I'd have been here sooner if we hadn't got held up in the High Street,' said Nelly, feeling that an explanation for her lateness was called for. 'A burst water main has sealed off the road in both directions. We had to go all round the houses to get here.'

Ig looked at Loo, excitedly. 'We've never been to the High Street, Nelly, it's too risky for us to go so far from the house, even in the winter.'

'We can't control the temperatures outside like we can in here,' explained Loo, pointing all three eyes in the direction of a pizza-sized thermostatic control switch, positioned centrally on the far wall.

'It has to be zero degrees or below at all times for us Thermitts!' smiled Ig.

Nelly smiled back and then shivered. Even with a wardrobe full of clothes on, a chilly nip was weedling its way into her bones.

'Have you ever been outside?' she asked, shuddering at the thought of what a heat wave would do to a Thermitt.

'Oh yes,' drawled Ig, 'but only as far as the back garden, and always in deepest winter.'

'The winter nights can be nice,' drawled Loo, joining Nelly on the sofa. 'On a cloudless night when the temperatures drop below freezing we can sometimes get out and about.'

'But only as far as the back fence,' cautioned Ig. 'It's too risky to go any further.'

Nelly pushed her bobble hat further up her forehead and then peeped over the rim of her scarves at Nip. This was a puzzle. As far as she had always understood, the basic idea of monster sitting was that she stayed in, while the monsters went out. But here she was at number 27 Blackjack Street, with two monster parents who couldn't possibly leave the house. Especially on a day like today.

'I don't understand,' said Nelly, deciding to confront the situation. 'If you can't go out of the house, why do you need me to monster sit?'

Loo looked at Ig and smiled.

'Ahaaaaaaa!' drawled Ig, punching the air

excitedly and skiiing across the icy floor on his
ski-length feet. 'Wait till you see what we've
bought!'

Loo curled the tip of her finger around Nelly's
wrist and beckoned her to follow. Nelly cradled
Nip in her arms and heaved herself up from the
icy cushions.

The light from the open lounge door provided
a floodlight for the hallway and as Nelly inched
her way tentatively through the doorway, she got
her clearest view of the hallway and staircase yet.

As she suspected, a white ice-rink carpet
stretched right up to the white enamelled front
door. Stranger than strange, though, was the
staircase.

To Nelly's amazement the stairs were completely
stairless. Instead of steps leading up to the first
floor of the house, a solid wedge of ice sloped
steeply upwards towards the landing. There was
no banister rail to hold on to and no cupboard
under the stairs. The Thermitts' staircase was
simply a giant, solid wedge of sparkling ice.

Nelly's eyes skiied inquisitively up the slope. At the top, hanging motionless from a steel track embedded into the ceiling, a chairlift seat sat waiting.

'Ig won't be long!' drawled Loo, following Nelly's gaze to the cloud of freezing fog that was swirling like mountain mist at the top of the stairs. 'He's just getting changed.'

Nelly ruffled Nip's hair fondly with her gloves and then slid her eyes to the bottom of the slope. The tops of two junior ski poles were poking like bulrushes from a heavy steel tubular container.

'Walking spikes,' drawled Loo. 'Nip used to use them when he was learning to walk. The spikes helped him steady himself on the ice, didn't they, Nip? When you were a little Nippybubba!'

Nip smiled adoringly back at his mum and then pointed up the stairs.

'Here he comes!' drawled Loo excitedly.

Nelly stared open mouthed at the landing.

A giant, silver-foiled potato was climbing into the chairlift. At least that's what it looked like.

For Ig was dressed from top to toe in a one-piece silver suit!

'Doesn't he look dashing?' drawled Loo, gazing adoringly up the slope.

Nelly nodded politely.

With a wave of his thickly-padded arm and a wiggle of his thickly-padded legs, Ig made a *Stars in Your Eyes* entrance through the swirling mist. The chairlift stopped at the bottom, allowing Ig to wriggle and prise his bottom free.

Nelly and Loo stepped to one side as the silver lump lurched towards them before regaining its normal grip on the ice.

'Wahdooink?' drawled Ig from inside the silver face mask.

Nelly stared blankly back at him and then turned to Loo for a translation.

Loo smiled and unzipped the mask to the height of Ig's seventh chin.

'WHAT DO YOU THINK?' drawled Ig, muffle-free this time. 'Shall I give you a twirl?'

Nelly laughed as Ig pirouetted like an ice skater

down the hallway and then snowploughed to a halt at the foot of the slope.

'Isn't it wonderful, Nelly? Isn't it chic?' he drawled.

The fabric of Ig's top to toe suit looked space age and beyond. Nelly raised her glove and gave it an exploratory poke with her finger. It had a pliant silver feel, but inside its padded ribbing there was the definite crunch of ice. If anything it reminded her of her Auntie Jane's wine cooler.

'It's made of Krystillin, Nelly,' said Loo. 'Krystillin is the very latest in thermal fabric design.'

'It's got crystals in,' drawled Ig, holding out his silver-padded sleeves, 'crystals of thermal ice that will freeze to minus twenty degrees and stay frozen, whatever the temperature outside of the suit!'

'You know what this means, don't you, Nelly?' said Loo with a wobble of excitement. 'It means Ig and I can go outside, even on a day like today!'

'We can go to the High Street for the first time, Nelly!' jiggled Ig.

'We've never seen a burst water main before!' drawled Loo.

'Unfortunately they don't make these suits in Nip's size, Nelly, so we aren't able to take him with us,' drawled Ig.

'I understand,' smiled Nelly, steaming the hallway with the warmth of her breath. 'And I'm sure Nip does too.'

Everything was clear now. Nelly *was* truly needed. The Thermitts *would* be leaving the house after all; leaving the house for the very first time in fact! She felt excited for Ig and Loo, although she wasn't sure that the burst water main was the perfect venue for a day trip. But hey, she wasn't a Thermitt. What a thrill it would be for them to step out into the summer sunshine for the first time!

'Don't you worry about Nip,' she said, cradling him in her arms. 'Nip and I will have a fantastic time while you're gone.'

'I'll go and put my suit on!' drawled Loo, climbing into the chairlift and pushing the button at the bottom of the slope.

'I can't wait to see you in it!' smiled Nelly.

7

Ig and Loo's Krystillin suits flashed like paparazzi cameras as they finally stepped outside into the bright summer sunshine. They looked like sumo astronauts as they lumbered hand in hand down the front path towards the pavement.

The intrepid pair paused for a moment at the end of the drive and then turned back towards Nelly and Nip to deliver two reassuring thumbs (or rather fingers) up. Nelly blew a kiss down the driveway on Nip's behalf and then closed the front door firmly behind them. A cloud of frozen air billowed back into the hallway as the freezer-style front door slotted into its airtight rubber seal with a swoosh.

Nelly blinked goodbye to the heat-wave sunshine and then peered through the half light at her feet. They were considerably shorter than French-bread loaves and not equipped for ice travel at all. Slowly and ever so slightly wobbily she carried Nip back to the lounge.

It was already quarter to two and she hadn't even played one game with the little fella yet. But Nip didn't seem to mind. He had completely taken to Nelly and was hugging tight to her chest like a koala.

Nelly decided to have a little look around.

The freezer theme continued throughout all the rooms at ground level. The kitchen walls were moulded from white preformed plastic and had the sparkling texture of a January frost. Work surfaces and units were sculpted from solid ice and a chopping board of sheet ice was scattered with icy shards.

Nelly ran the tip of her gloved finger across the icing of frost that caked the window to the back garden.

Sunlight sliced through the narrow slit that she had made on the pane. Nelly peered through at the garden. It was a swimming pool from front to back! A shallow paddle in the summer months, an ice rink in the winter.

'Is that where you go to play when the temperatures are cold enough, Nippy?' said Nelly, holding the Thermitt up to her eye level.

Nip nodded and then buried himself in her puffa jacket again.

With a wobble and a teeter, Nelly turned herself round and inched her way out of the kitchen and into the Thermitts' back room. There was an ice-sculpted dining table in the centre of the room with two high-backed ice chairs either end. The table was set, not with cutlery, but with ice picks, and a large glass salt cruet, full to the brim with pink road grit, stood at the very centre.

Nip's highchair stood glistening against the far wall beneath a signed and framed photograph of a Himalayan yeti. Nelly inched nearer and peered at the caption.

It read, 'To Ig and Loo. Lots of love from your Great Uncle Lurge.'

'So yetis are real!' gasped Nelly, prising Nip from her chest. Nip looked up at her and triple blinked. He hadn't yet had the pleasure of meeting his extremely distant relative.

'I knew they were real,' said Nelly. 'If I ever go to the Himalayas, I'll do some monster sitting there, too!'

As she turned away from the framed picture her attention was drawn to a galvanised-steel box tucked tidily away in the corner of the room. Although the box itself was silver-grey in colour, the large Edam-shaped objects inside gave the room a rare splash of bright colour.

'Curling stones!' she cried. 'I've always wanted to have a go at curling!'

Nelly was right – it was a box of green and red curling stones. A most appropriate hobby for a Thermitt!

Nelly knew precisely what to do with them, having watched the Winter Olympics curling final on telly from start to finish.

She guessed the Thermitts probably played

with them outdoors when the back garden froze solid in the winter, but, hey, Nelly was a resourceful girl. She was sure she could put them to good use in the lounge!

'Do you mind if I put you down, Nippy?' said Nelly. 'I'm going to need my arms to balance.'

Nip relaxed his asparagus-green fingers and allowed Nelly to lower him to the floor. Although he couldn't talk, he could most certainly walk. And skate and glide and triple salchow. Nelly watched with amusement as Nip circled the table twice before gliding to a halt beside the box of curling stones.

'You'll have to give me skiing lessons!' Nelly laughed, tottering over to the corner and lifting out two stones. 'Follow me, Nippy,' said Nelly, almost losing her balance and toppling on to her bottom. 'Mind these don't fall on your head!'

Nip kept his distance as Nelly made her way back into the Thermitts' lounge with the curling stones. They were much heavier than she had imagined, and boy was she pleased to finally drop them on to the sofa. The stones crunched into the cushions with a thud and a clack then slid to the centre of the middle seat.

'We'll only use one to start off with,' said Nelly, lifting a bright-red curling stone from the box.

Nip stood quietly by the sofa as Nelly lowered the curling stone on to the icy floor and then closed her fingers around its handle.

'Watch me, Nippy,' said Nelly, peeping over the rim of her scarves and aiming the stone at the bay window. 'This is what we do, Nippy,' she continued, giving the curling stone the gentlest of pushes with her thickly-padded arm.

Nip watched as the red curling stone slid across the lounge's ice-rink floor. With a kick of his ski-length feet, he set off in pursuit. By the time the curling stone had reached the far wall Nip was there to greet it.

'Now you see if you can push it to me!' said Nelly, dropping to her knees and clapping her gloves together encouragingly.

Nip smiled shyly across the lounge floor in the direction of Nelly.

Spurred on by another woolly clap of encouragement he placed both of his green fingers either side of the stone and pushed with all his might.

The handle spun anticlockwise as the curling stone made spiralling but icy-smooth progress across the glassy finish of the floor.

Nelly leaned forward as best she could to receive it, gathering it into the folds of her puffa jacket with her gloves.

'Well done, Nippy,' said Nelly, prising her

bobble hat up over her ears. 'I'll make a curling champion of you yet!'

Nip stayed silent but seemed visibly excited as Nelly hooked her arm around a leg of the lolly-stick table and crept on all fours across the ice.

'Now then, Nippy, stay where you are and see if you can aim the stone right through the legs of the table without touching the sides. A point to you if you can, a point to me if you can't!'

Nip watched inquisitively as Nelly positioned the lolly-stick table in the centre of the room before scrabbling back on all fours towards the settee.

'Me first!' she said, kneeling on the frozen floor and aiming carefully at the lolly-stick goalposts. The curling stone left her gloves and glided straight and true across the ice.

'Bull's-eye! One point to me!' laughed Nelly, peeling her bobble hat further up her forehead. 'Now it's your turn, Nippy.'

Nip positioned his fingers either side of the curling stone again and aimed a little less expertly.

With an excited lunge the stone spun diagonally across the floor, clipping the right-hand table leg before ricocheting left towards goal.

Nelly lurched one way then the other, finally gathering the handle of the stone into the woolly fingers of her right glove.

'I'll give you that,' she said generously. 'One point each. My go again.'

And so the game continued, with Nip sending the stone erratically across the floor in all directions and Nelly generously compensating for his inaccuracy by missing on purpose. It wasn't Olympic-standard curling by any stretch of the imagination but Nip was having fun and for Nelly that was all that mattered.

It wasn't until after the eleventh curl, with the score at 6–5 in Nip's favour, that the game took a turn for the worse.

Nip released the twelfth stone in Nelly's direction in much the same way that he had released all the others. His three orange eyes had focused hard, his lips had nibbled excitedly and his blubbery little arms had pushed as best they could. But as the curling stone spiralled across the ice towards the left-hand leg of the lolly-stick table, it suddenly sank through the floor!

Nelly rubbed her eyes. But she wasn't mistaken. The curling stone had sunk without a trace!

She scrambled to her feet, but as she threw her weight forward, her knees crunched through the ice.

'Oh no,' gasped Nelly.

The lounge floor was melting!

8

It was still chilly in the house, but it wasn't zero degrees or below. Nelly looked round at the thermostat on the wall. It was two degrees above zero!

She looked down at her feet and winced. She was ankle deep in crushed ice.

'It has to be zero or below for us Thermitts.' That was what Ig had said. But what did he mean exactly? What would happen to a Thermitt if the temperature rose above zero degrees? Nelly looked anxiously at Nip. She was about to find out.

Nip was still staring disbelievingly at the centre of the lounge floor, trying to fathom where the curling stone had disappeared to. He appeared to be OK from the outside at least – potatoey, blubbery, Thermitty – but as he tried to stand up on the ice Nelly began to fear the worst.

Nip's balance had gone. Although light enough in body weight not to crack the ice beneath him, his little baguette-length feet slid waywardly in all directions as he tried to ease himself up.

Nelly half skated, half crunched her way across the floor and scooped the toddler into her arms.

'It's OK, Nippy, don't you worry – Nelly will fix it,' said Nelly, cradling Nip over to the sofa and laying him down. But there was more bad news. The cushions were melting too.

Nelly shivered, more with horror than with cold. The entire house seemed to be defrosting fast, but how, and why? And more importantly, how was she going to stop it?

She flashed her eyes upwards to the ceiling light and then wheeled around towards the hallway door. With three crunching bounds she wrapped her gloves around the long, plastic handle and wrenched the door free from its rubber seal.

A small wave of icy water lapped around her ankles. The hallway was defrosting too. Nelly looked up at the ceiling of the lounge again and opened and closed the door.

Things were worse than she thought. The fridge-style door was opening all right but the neon-bright lightbulb light in the room wasn't working. That could only mean one thing.

'A fuse must have blown,' groaned Nelly, whose electrical know-how stopped there. 'What am I going to do now?'

She knew nothing about fuses or fuse boxes.

'Where is Mummy and Daddy's fuse box, Nippy? Can you tell Nelly where it is?'

Nip looked up from the sofa with pale, lemon-coloured eyes. He knew less than nothing about electrics and was in no condition to share the nothing he didn't know, either.

Nelly wrenched open the door of the lounge again and strode through the darkness of the hall

towards the front door. Gripping the handle of
the door with both hands she prepared to tug,
and then stopped.

She was snookered. She couldn't go for
help because that would mean leaving Nip alone
in the house. And she couldn't take him with
her because the heat wave outside would kill
him.

'I'll ring Dad!' she gasped, plunging her hand
towards her jeans pocket but finding herself
repelled by a puffa jacket, overcoat and sweatshirt.
After a wild, fumbling frenzy of woollen fingers,
zips and buttons she finally thrust her mobile
phone to her ear.

'Hi, Mum, is Dad there?' she chimed, trying to
sound as composed as she possibly could.

There was a pause.

'Hi, Dad, fine thanks,' Nelly fibbed. 'Yes, I'm
having a lovely time, thanks.'

There was a sneeze.

'Hayfever got you again, eh, Dad? Dad,
whereabouts in a house would I be likely to find a

fuse box?' said Nelly, deciding to stop footsying around.

Nelly's face dropped.

'In the cupboard under the stairs?' she groaned. 'But the Thermitts haven't got a cupboard under the stairs! THEY HAVEN'T EVEN GOT STAIRS!'

Nelly lowered her mobile from her ear and then sprung it back fast.

'WHAT?' she squeaked. 'BUT THERE CAN'T BE! THERE MUSTN'T BE!'

But there was.

Nelly's dad had delivered a bombshell.

Nelly was wasting her time looking for fuses or fuse boxes. Her mum and dad had no electricity either. Their fans weren't working, the microwave clock was blinking, the telly was pictureless, the radio was tuneless. In fact, the whole of the Montelimar Estate had been without electricity for half an hour at least.

The workmen in the High Street were to blame. They had fractured the water pipe trying to repair it, shorted the underground electricity cables and landed the entire Montelimar Estate with a full-scale power cut.

Nelly stood motionless for a moment, her toes numb with cold and her socks soggy with slush.

'Ice. I need ice. I NEED ALL THE ICE YOU'VE GOT, DAD, AND I NEED IT. NOW!'

There was a sneeze, a pause, another sneeze and an apology.

Her dad had tipped all their ice into the ice bucket earlier that day and it had long since

melted in the sunshine. There wasn't any ice at number 119, Sweet Street and if the power cut lasted much longer there wouldn't be any at 27 Blackjack Street either!

'But it's a matter of LIFE AND DEATH!' cried Nelly.

There was a pause, another pause and then suddenly another pause.

Nelly thrust her mobile into her puffa-jacket pocket and waded through the meltwaters back to the lounge. This was getting serious. She needed some monster help. So did Nip. The tips of his fingers had turned white and the folds in his skin were beginning to wrinkle.

I'll ring Splat and Dollop, she thought. No. They'd get into too much of a froth in this heat.

I could ring Grit and Blob, but they don't have a freezer.

Nelly piled what was left of the icy sofa cushions around Nip and then sprinkled him with slush from the floor. His lemon eyes responded with a grateful blink.

'I'll ring directory enquiries!' she blurted, tapping her phone pad urgently with her gloves.

There was a pause and a 'How may I help you?'

'Ice deliveries, please. Can you text me the number of every ice-cube delivery company in the area, please,' said Nelly.

'What is your area?' asked the woman on the other end of the phone.

'Europe,' said Nelly, not wanting to narrow her chances.

But the whole of Europe was out of ice cubes. In fact the heat wave was so widespread even Great Uncle Lurge in the Himalayas was probably running low.

Nelly was getting desperate. Nip was getting weaker. Time was of the essence. There must be someone she could ring. She scrolled through her address book to see which of her monster friends lived closest to the Thermitts.

It was the Gloobles at 78, Menthol Way. Menthol Way was only three streets away which meant if they had ice cubes Grilse could run round with them in a matter of seconds. They definitely had a freezer, because the first time she had babysat for them Nelly had defrosted the children's jov burgers by mistake before feeding them. (Gloobles always eat their food frozen.)

Nelly tapped out their number and held her breath.

There was a squeak, a chiffachaffa and a hello?

'Grilse, it's Nelly! Have you got any ice cubes? I need some ICE CUBES NOW!'

There was a chiffachaffa, a squeak and a 'VILE? IT'S NELLY! SHE NEEDS SOME ICE CUBES! HAVE WE GOT ANY LEFT IN THE FREEZER OR HAVE THEY ALL MELTED?'

Nelly waited for the decibels to drop and then pressed her mobile phone back against her ear.

'ALL OUR ICE CUBES ARE MELTING, NELLY,' squeaked Grilse. 'THERE'S A POWER CUT, YOU KNOW.'

Nelly sighed. 'Have you got anything at all that's frozen?' she asked. 'I'm desperate.'

There was a pause, a rummage and then a slam of a freezer door.

'THREE PACKETS OF FROZEN WEEPS,' squeaked Grilse. 'BUT THEY'RE DEFROSTING FAST.'

It was better than nothing.

'CAN YOU BRING THEM ROUND PLEASE, GRILSE?' begged Nelly. 'I'M JUST ROUND THE CORNER AT NUMBER 27, BLACKJACK STREET. IT'S AN EMERGENCY!'

There was a 'RIGHT AWAY!' and a click.

Nelly returned her mobile to her puffa-jacket pocket and stared anxiously at Nip. The cushions he was lying on were half their original size now and the filling inside the freezer-block sofa was thawing to an icy slush.

Nip looked desperately tired. The blubbery folds of his skin had wrinkled like new Plasticine, his arms were limp, his fingers were white and his eyelids were drooping.

'Help is on the way, Nippy,' whispered Nelly, packing some more icy slush around his chest.

Nelly was kidding herself. Three packets of frozen weeps were on their way, that was all. What possible use would they be? The temperature on the thermostat had risen to six degrees. The lounge floor was wall to wall Slush Puppy. Things were about as bad as they could get, worse if you were a Thermitt.

The doorbell rang. Nelly leapt from the sofa and waded through the icy shallows of the hall. When she wrenched the door open she found Grilse panting wildly on the doorstep, holding a packet of frozen weeps in each claw.

'This is all that's left of the ice cubes,' he squeaked apologetically, holding up a clear polythene bag of warm water with his fourth paw. 'It's SO hot outside today, Nelly. That's why everything in the freezer is melting so fast!'

Nelly ushered him inside. 'I need to close the door quickly, Grilse,' she explained, 'before the temperature in here rises any further!'

Grilse stepped into the hallway and shuddered as the icy meltwaters crept between the furry tufts of his toes. 'You *have* got an emergency, haven't you?' he squeaked, lifting his tails from the icy depths and tying them like string around his waist.

'Follow me,' said Nelly. 'The light is better in the lounge.'

Grilse trailed through the slush of the dark hallway and followed Nelly through to the lounge.

'Oh dear,' he chiffachaffered. 'You're not a well Thermitt at all, are you?'

Nip turned away shyly as Grilse sat down on the sofa and tried to place a comforting claw on his forehead. Nelly prised the frozen weep packets from his other paws and placed them like a duvet across Nip's chest and waist. The weeps inside the packets were barely frozen at all now, but at least they made Nelly feel as though she was doing something useful.

'It's still pretty cold in here, Nelly,' whispered Grilse optimistically. 'Are you sure there isn't any more ice in the house?'

'I haven't been upstairs,' said Nelly. 'Maybe

there's a supply of ice in the bedrooms upstairs!'

Her hopes rose and then plummeted. The chairlift wouldn't be going anywhere without electricity.

'There's the kitchen table and chairs in the back room,' remembered Nelly. 'They're made of ice. I'm sure they won't have melted yet.'

'Then why don't we take Nip into the back room? We can lie him down on the table.'

Nelly brightened immediately. It was a good idea, and good ideas were in short supply at the moment. Grilse tried to lift Nip into his paws but a whimper of protest made it clear that Nip only wanted Nelly to carry him.

Nelly scooped him up, weep packets and all, and waded though to the back room.

The dining-room table had somewhat lost its shape. The legs had melted to coffee-table height but there was still enough of the icy table top remaining to provide Nip with an impromptu hospital bed.

Nelly laid him down carefully and nibbled her lip. She was doing her best for him but it didn't feel nearly enough. Grilse placed a claw on Nelly's thickly padded shoulder and gave her a consoling cuddle.

'I'm sorry I can't be of more help, Nelly – it's this infernal heat wave we're having.'

Nelly peered at the back window. The frosty white coating had melted away and the panes were crystal clear. She stared silently for a moment at the sunshine in the garden and then wheeled round towards the lounge door.

She could hear something. A soft but tuneful tinkle-tankling, growing louder and louder and louder. An ice-cream van was turning into Blackjack Street!

'Look after Nip!' cried Nelly, racing out of the back room, through the slush of the lounge and down the icy waters of the hall. Placing both gloves tightly around the handle she wrenched the front door open. The sunshine blinded her for a moment but to her delight, when she opened her eyes she found the ice-cream van had pulled up directly outside.

With a whoop and a wave she leaped the front step and waddled headlong into the heat-wave sunshine. Despite all her layers of clothes she was still first to the front of the queue.

'What'll it be, lov—' The ice-cream man's jaw locked in mid sentence as he turned slowly from the chocolate flakes in his freezer cabinet to find a three-scarved, two-gloved, bobble-hatted nutcase peering up at him from the pavement.

'Harmucchherthechokises?' said Nelly, finding it hard to speak clearly through her scarves.

Beads of perspiration trickled through the ice-cream man's wispy sideburns as he threw a startled look towards the other children in the queue.

Nelly raised her thickly padded arms and pulled her scarves clear of her lips.

'HOW MUCH ARE THE CHOC ICES?' she asked again.

The ice-cream man looked round at his freezer box and then managed to find his voice.

'Fifty pence,' he whispered hoarsely.

'I'LL HAVE FIFTY, PLEASE,' said Nelly, flapping her overcoat and puffa jacket open with her arm.

The queue of T-shirted children behind her groaned and then backed up to create more space for Nelly's next multi-layered manoeuvre: a tricky little exercise called 'getting your money out of your pocket'.

The ice-cream man placed an unopened box of choc ices on the counter and then watched in disbelief as Nelly thrashed and staggered to and fro in the sunshine, trying to bend her thickly padded arms far enough back to reach her pocket. Finally, with a lunge and a Huffaluk growl she wrenched her twenty-five pounds free.

'Cheers a lot!' she said, slapping her lottery winnings down on the ice-cream man's knuckles and reaching the choc-ice box down from the counter.

'Make way!' she shouted, scattering the ice-cream queue in all directions and stomping like an over-dressed elephant back to the Thermitts' front door.

She had left the door ever so slightly ajar and with a nudge of her considerably large bum she was soon sloshing down the hallway with the choc-ice box in hand.

'Look, Nippy!' she cried as she splashed into the back room. 'Building bricks! Would you like to play building bricks with Nelly!'

Grilse sliced the choc-ice box open with his middle claw and helped to lift the choc ices out. 'These smell delicious!' he slavered. 'Can I try one?'

'No you can't,' said Nelly, who wouldn't have minded one herself. 'They're all for Nippy.'

Nip smiled weakly and tried to sit up, but his toddler playfulness had deserted him.

'Howsabout you lie there, Nippy, and we'll build an igloo around you?' said Nelly.

320

Nippy peeped up from his duvet of soggy weep packets and blinked a grateful OK.

Nelly and Grilse began brick laying, placing each choc ice in turn close to the poorly Thermitt's body. The effects were immediate. Nip's eyes darkened from pale lemon to light orange and the tips of his fingers flushed with just the hint of asparagus green.

'It's helping,' whispered Nelly. 'It's helping just a little.'

'How are we going to build the roof?' squeaked Grilse, laying his first choc ice of the fourth course.

The question didn't require an answer. There weren't enough choc ices for a roof.

By the time the igloo wall had been laid three times around Nip's body the choc-ice box was completely empty.

Nelly peered hopefully over her side of the wall, looking for more signs of recovery.

Nip was no worse, but he was no better either.

She gingerly prodded the choc ice that was closest to her chin. The chocolate coating cracked inside the wrapper. The choc ices were melting now.

Nelly closed her eyes and turned towards the far wall. The top of Nip's highchair was melting through the floor. She stared down at her feet. The icy meltwaters were lapping around her knees now. She dreaded to think what the kitchen units looked like.

If only Ig and Loo would return home. They could pick Nippy up and tuck him inside the zip of a Krystillin suit. He would perfectly safe inside there. But there was no sign of Ig or Loo. They could be anywhere. If they knew there was a power cut Nelly was sure they would have returned home.

Nelly sighed deeply and then looked at the portrait of Great Uncle Lurge. If only he could tell her what to do. But the snowbound hillsides of the Himalayan mountains were a far cry from the frostless plastic walls of the Thermitts' home. There was simply nothing else that she could do.

Where could she get electricity from if there was no electricity? Where could she get ice from if there was no ice? Where could she get cold from if there was no cold? Nelly gulped. If the temperature rose one more degree, Nip would be done for.

What could she do? What could she do? She didn't have a Krystillin suit. All she had was some soggy choc ices, a bag of warm water and three packets of defrosted weeps.

She looked at the weeps.

She stared at the weeps.

She thought about the weeps.

'Weeps . . . weep pods . . . Hallowe'en masks . . . curtains!' she gasped. 'I'll ring the Muggots! Maybe Leafmould will be able to save us!'

Grilse watched, puzzled, as Nelly plucked the mobile from her puffa-jacket pocket and raised it to her ear.

'Hello? Leafmould? It's Nelly! Leafmould – am I pleased to speak to you!'

There was a gullop, a snuffle and an extremely long pause as Nelly explained her idea.

'. . . So I need sub-zero temperatures,

Leafmould, and I need them right now in this very room. All over the house, actually. Please, Leafmould, you must help me. I don't mind how much it costs to hire them again, I'll cut your lawns every week and you can have all my pocket money for a year, just make the phone call, please!' pleaded Nelly.

'Nelly, I'll do what I can,' said Leafmould, 'but I'm not sure if they do afternoon appearances. All our bookings were for midnight.'

'Then persuade them, Leafmould. PLEASE, PERSUADE THEM!' begged Nelly.

'I most certainly *will* persuade them, Nelly,' said Leafmould. 'And don't you worry about the hire costs, I will pay for them myself. The Muggots of Badley Hall are for ever in your debt, Nelly, you know that. How are you, by the way?'

Nelly's toes curled tightly inside her soggy trainers. 'Make the phone call NOW, Leafmould!'

There was a snoffle, a snuffle, a 'Right away, Nelly' and a click.

'What do we do now, Nelly?' asked Grilse.

Nelly slipped her mobile phone inside her pocket and placed her glove tenderly on Nippy's wrinkled forehead.

'We wait,' murmured Nelly. 'All we can do is wait.'

9

'Bang bang bang!' went the front door.

'Who's that?' asked Grilse, hoicking the tips of his tails higher up out of the icy water.

'Ig and Loo, I hope,' said Nelly, crossing her fingers and wading as hard as she could through to the lounge and into the hallway.

She threw the open the doorway but to her surprise was confronted by her dad.

'Dad! What are you doing here?' she said. 'It isn't four o'clock already is it?'

'No, it's quarter to three. But you sounded desperate,' he said, handing Nelly another polythene bag of warm water.

'I am desperate, Dad,' she said, ushering him in through the door. 'Mind your—

'Step,' she winced, as her dad's Jesus sandals

disappeared into the icy depths of the hallway floor.

Nelly's dad shuddered and then lurched forward with his arms flapping.

'What the—!' he cried, managing to regain his balance at the other end of the hall.

'There's a power cut here too!' sighed Nelly.

Nelly led her shivering dad through to the back room and introduced him to Grilse and Nippy.

Reassured by the absence of both cobwebs and spiders, Nelly's dad listened to the events leading up to the phone call that Nelly had made to the Muggots of Badley Hall.

'So now we wait,' said Nelly.

'Wait for what?' asked her dad.

'You'll see,' smiled Nelly. 'Actually, maybe you won't see them at all!'

Nelly was right. There was nothing they could see. But there was something they could feel. Within minutes of making the call to Leafmould, the temperature in the back room of the house suddenly and inexplicably plummeted.

Nelly's dad's nipples tightened, his arms bristled with goosebumps and the sweat on his T-shirt turned to ice.

Nelly looked towards Grilse with a wink. 'They're here!' she said.

Grilse's teeth began to chatter. 'Has the power come back on?'

Nelly shook her head. 'Keep moving your feet, or your legs will set solid in the ice.'

Nelly's dad looked down at his feet. His bare legs were numb and ice crystals were beginning to form around the hairs on his knees.

'Let's sit on the windowsill,' said Nelly, lifting Nippy from the table and cradling him in her arms. 'We'll be out of the way there.'

Nelly's dad turned towards the window and jumped.

'*Something just blew down my T-shirt!*' he stammered.

'*And something just tugged the knots in my tail!*' shivered Grilse.

'They're only playing,' laughed Nelly, boosted

328

by the rapidly-improving colour of Nippy's eyes.

'Who are only playing?' squeaked Grilse, wheeling round as another puff of arctic air whistled into his ear.

'The ghosts of Badley Hall,' smiled Nelly. 'Or should I say, the *former* ghosts of Badley Hall. Leafmould used to hire them to haunt Riggll and Rythe. They used to fill their bedroom with cold spots!'

'It's f-f-f-f-freezing in here, Nelly,' chattered her dad, prising the ice crystals from his knees.

'If you need some cold spots, then get some ghosts!' laughed Nelly, lifting Nippy's satsuma-orange eyes to hers and giving him a kiss.

'I don't like ghosts,' said Nelly's dad nervously, stepping back down on to the fast freezing floor and crunching his way towards the lounge door.

Before he could reach the handle, the door opened by itself, forcing a tidal wave of icy slush to ride up around his frozen knees. Nelly's dad's jaw dropped open as a red curling stone floated into the room at head height and began circling his head. It was followed by a green curling stone and a lolly-stick table.

'Look, Nippy!' smiled Nelly. 'Some poltergeists have come to play!'

Nippy lifted his head and smiled. His wrinkles had begun to disappear now and a healthy sub-zero chill was returning to his veins.

Nelly's dad bobbed and weaved as the two curling stones began spiralling around his head.

'I'm off!' he said, striding into the lounge and lunging for the door handle that led to the hallway.

To his horror, two giant apparitions reached the hallway door before he could and wrenched it open from the other side. Bursting into the lounge from the darkness of the hallway, they loomed straight towards him. Nelly's dad yelled. They were huge, they were terrifying, they had bright orange eyes and the humungous blobby appearance of giant, silver potatoes.

Ig and Loo had returned!

'Neeee!' they cried, their voices muffled by the full-face padding of their silver head masks.

Nelly's dad began back-pedalling fast as the two giant, silver lumps came bowling through the lounge towards him. Ice splintered around the back of his knees and slush flew up the legs of his shorts as he reversed like a speedboat back in the direction he had come.

Nelly jumped down from the window ledge with Nip in her arms and crunched through the ice to greet the Thermitts. With a rasp of zips and a crunch and a splash, Ig and Loo removed their Krystillin hoods and Nelly's dad toppled backwards into the slush.

Nelly didn't know which way to turn first. Fortunately, Grilse was on hand to help out. As he pulled Nelly's dad up from the fast freezing floor, Nelly passed Nip into Ig's outstretched arms.

'We came as soon as we realised, Nelly!' drawled Loo. 'Please forgive us for taking so long.'

Nelly watched with relief as Ig unzipped his

Krystillin suit and cocooned Nippy safely inside.

'What a mess!' said Loo, surveying the melted remains of her furniture, not to mention the flotsam and jetsam of weep packets, choc-ice wrappers and lolly sticks. 'It's a miracle that Nip has survived.'

'Sometimes miracles happen!' smiled Nelly, wrapping her puffa jacket around her dad's shoulders.

'You can say that again,' said Ig, as two curling stones floated through the air into the kitchen and lowered themselves back into their box.

Nelly crunched across the ice, and wrenched open the door. The neon bright lightbulb in the centre of the ceiling blinked into life, throwing a blinding fluorescence across the room.

'The electricity is back on!' smiled Nelly, waving thanks to her invisible spirit helpers.

'Then I will go and fetch the snow shovel,' drawled Loo.

As much as Grilse and Nelly's dad would have liked to have helped to tidy up, they weren't dressed for arctic conditions at all. The knot in Grilse's tail had already frozen fast and Nelly's dad's nose was about to drop off from frostbite. Both bade teeth-chattering farewells and went outside to thaw out in the sunshine.

Nelly stayed indoors to help re-level the floors and chip the remains of the furniture into bin bags. She had promised she would stay until four, and a promise was a promise as far as Nelly was concerned.

'Not to worry. We can buy a new kitchen,' drawled Loo, 'and table and chairs.'

'The important thing is that Nip is all right,' said Ig, looking tenderly down at his son, who was curled happily into the cavity of his Krystillin suit. 'Thank goodness you stopped the temperature from rising.'

Nelly propped the snow shovel handle next to Great Uncle Lurge and stood back to survey the floor. It was firm underfoot now and with a bit of polishing would soon be ice-rink smooth once again.

'Let's see how you are, little fella,' said Ig, pulling Nip out from his suit and lowering him gently to the ice. Nip's feet scissored in two directions and his fingers flapped at the air.

'He's a little unsteady still,' drawled Loo. 'I'll go and get his walking spikes.'

As Loo left the room, Nelly sat down on the floor with a sigh. The padding from her jeans and overcoat kept the chill from her bottom and her bobble hat and scarves kept the tingle from her nose. She didn't need to look at the thermostat to know that the temperature had returned to zero or below. What a crazy three hours it had been!

'Here you are, Nip,' drawled Loo, returning from the hallway, minus her suit and holding two small walking spikes.

Nip reached up, took the walking spikes from his mother, and began slaloming expertly around the floor.

'I wish I could ski like that!' laughed Nelly, clapping encouragingly with her gloves.

Nip skiied towards her with a smile and then whizzed full circle around the room.

'What's that stuck to Nip's walking spike?' said Nelly with a squint.

Ig and Loo looked down at the ice and followed their son's progress around the room.

'It's a piece of paper, I think,' drawled Ig. 'He probably picked it up when he was playing in the back garden last winter.'

Nelly squinted again at the small piece of paper impaled on the tip of Nip's ski pole.

'Can I see please, Nippy?' she said, opening her arms wide.

Nip glided across the floor and slid softly into Nelly's arms. Nelly ruffled his hair and then examined the spike.

There was definitely a piece of litter impaled on the tip of the pole. Nelly pulled it off and then gasped.

Miracle of miracles. It was Mrs Lavender's lottery ticket!

10

If her dad hadn't had the car Nelly would have run the two miles back to her home, heat wave or no heat wave.

When she knocked on Mrs Lavender's door at quarter-past four that afternoon her heart was inside her mouth.

'I've found your lottery ticket!' she blurted, as Mrs Lavender opened her door.

Mrs Lavender leaned heavily on her walking stick, as wobbly on her door mat as Nip had been on the ice. Was it true? Had Nelly really answered her prayers? She looked through her spectacles at the ticket that Nelly was waving in front of her nose and then she peered to the end of the garden path. Nelly's mum and dad, her sister and three smiling monsters were standing by the hedge, happy to confirm that – hip hip hooray – it was true!

'I don't know how I can ever thank you enough,' she said, her eyes filling up with tears. 'Please, please, Nelly, let me share my winnings with you as a reward!'

Nelly shook her head and stepped back with a smile. 'That's very kind, Mrs Lavender, but I want you to keep your money. After all, I'm Nelly the Monster Sitter and being Nelly the Monster Sitter is like winning the lottery every day!'